VENEER

STORIES BY STEVE YARBROUGH

UNIVERSITY OF MISSOURI PRESS
Columbia and London

Library of Congress Cataloging-in-Publication Data

Yarbrough, Steve, 1956–
   Veneer : stories / by Steve Yarbrough.
      p.   cm.
   ISBN 0-8262-1185-2 (pbk. : alk. paper)
   I. Title
PS3575.A717V4   1998
813'.54—dc21   98-23152
                                         CIP

⊗ This paper meets the requirements of the
American National Standard for Permanence of Paper
for Printed Library Materials, Z39.48, 1984.

Designer: Mindy Shouse
Typesetter: Crane Typesetting
Printer and Binder: Thomson-Shore, Inc.
Typefaces: Berkeley Book, Empire

"The Lady Luck" first appeared in *American Short Fiction,* "The Rest of
Her Life" in *Missouri Review,* "Bohemia" in *Other Voices,* "Veneer" in
Oxford American, "Rottweiler" in *Quarterly West,* "Angel, Hold Your
Horses" in *Southern Review,* and "The Warsaw Voice" in *Tampa
Review.*

"Sleet" first appeared in *The Hudson Review.*

For James Lee Burke

For their help and encouragement, I would like to thank
Shana Eddy, Jessica Green, Sloan Harris, Beverly Jarrett, Marc Smirnoff,
Dabney Stuart, Clair Willcox, and the National Endowment for the Arts.

Contents

VENEER

The Lady Luck

IT'S FRIDAY afternoon, and they're through shooting. They pull into the parking lot, one after another, driving a whole string of Mercedes and Jags and BMWs. I didn't even know you could rent those kinds of cars. They didn't get them from Budget.

Our maintenance man, a young black guy named Lamon Collins, is sitting in the lobby, watching the sports on *Headline News*. When the cars start pulling in, he shakes his head. "Friday night," he says. "Gone be some damage done this evening."

He's no longer counting the days till the movie people leave, he could tell you how many minutes are involved. He says they've done stuff to the rooms a high school football team wouldn't do. The other night Charles Rhett got mad at the woman he had in his Jacuzzi. He told her to get out. She refused, so he grabbed the ice bucket and began emptying the Jacuzzi, a gallon at a time, dumping the water on the bathroom floor, just the sort of thing you'd expect him to do in one of his movies. It flooded

1

the whole suite. Lamon says the carpet there's ruined, and this morning he noticed that down next to the floor, the Sheetrock's growing pulpy, dissolving. I'm keeping strict tabs on the damages. I asked the owner if he wanted to consider eviction, but he thinks just knowing the movie people stayed here will make a lot of other folks want to spend the night.

I wouldn't count on that happening. Indianola's still Indianola. Back when we first opened up, the owner ordered me to position myself at the intersection of 49 and 82, at five on a Friday afternoon, and stop the first car I saw with non-Sunflower County plates. I was supposed to offer a free weekend stay in one of our executive suites. I'll bet I stopped fifty cars. I didn't find any takers until almost nine that night, and then it was just an old couple from Itta Bena. They'd gone over to one of the floating casinos in Greenville and lost a few quarters in the slot machines, and they seemed to think spending the night in Indianola was the perfect ending to a daring adventure.

"Whatever they tear up tonight," I tell Lamon, "I'm not going to ask you to fix it till Monday."

Lamon stands up and jams his hands in his pockets. Behind him, in the fireplace, the gas flames flicker. It's not cool enough yet for a fire, but the owner says it makes the place look warm and inviting.

"You'll be calling me," Lamon says. "Folks like these, man, when they want something, they want it now." He picks up his windbreaker, which has been lying on the back of his chair. "You ever wonder, Bob, what it'd be like to be rich? Ever ask yourself what you'd do with a million dollars?"

That kind of question always unnerves me. Telling the truth will erect an immediate barrier between me and the person asking the question. Lying will erect another sort of barrier.

But when you get right down to it, the question's really about cost—the cost of not being rich. So I lie. Because for me, in the end, lying's cheaper.

"Yeah, I wonder about it from time to time," I say. "But wondering won't do much good, will it?"

"Hasn't done me no good at all," Lamon says. "I'll spend the rest of my life pouring sulfuric acid down toilets to dissolve rubbers."

He leaves. I sit there on the stool, watching traffic pass on 82, glancing every now and then at the wall clock. My night clerk's been late the last two nights, and this is my anniversary. I've promised to take Betty out to eat in Greenville.

Finally the night clerk shows up. I'm walking out the door when I see Charles Rhett. He's coming toward me on the sidewalk.

You'd expect a fellow like him to be wearing something striking—clear plastic pants, say, or a pair of leather boots made from the hide of Secretariat—but he's got on faded Levis and a black sweatshirt and Reeboks that could stand to be cleaned. He waves at me. "Bob," he says. "Hey, Bob."

We've talked two or three times in the lobby, in the mornings when he comes in for his coffee and danish. He's the only one who eats the free continental breakfast. The others are having theirs catered. A van drives up from Jackson every morning.

"Got a second?" Rhett says.

"Sure."

The next thing I know, we're strolling along toward the green board fence that separates our parking lot from a junkyard. Rhett sets the pace. You can tell he's used to people walking just as slow—or just as fast—as he does.

"I'm real sorry," he says, "about fucking up that room the other night."

He's a Southerner himself, and right now he sounds like it, maybe because he's playing a Mississippian in the movie they're filming.

"I wouldn't have done it," he says, "if I'd been straight. I probably haven't shared this with you, but I've got this little substance problem."

Man-to-man talks are one thing I hate. Most of the ones I've taken part in involved my father. He did all the talking, and I did all the listening, except for one time, and that one time was a disaster.

Hoping to end this man-to-man talk fast, I try a joke. "All my problems," I tell Rhett, "have substance."

"I'm serious, Bob," he says. He stops walking and looks me in the eye. I remember a movie he played in. He was a Philadelphia cop, and he looked at some drug-dealing lowlife the same way, right before he stuck the barrel of his .45 in the lowlife's mouth and said, "Suck it, or the sun'll rise tomorrow on a world that won't include you."

I don't know what to say to him now. "Well," I finally manage, "I appreciate you telling me. I'll still have to charge somebody for the damages, though."

"You charge me," he says. "I'm the responsible party."

He turns, and I turn, and we're headed back toward the motel.

"It may happen again," he says. "I can't honestly tell you it won't."

"We could just drain the Jacuzzi," I offer. "That way, you wouldn't be subject to temptation."

"I'd find something else," he says. He steps on an unlucky roach. We stop long enough for him to grind it to paste with his Reebok. "That's one thing you can count on," he says. "I will sure find some way to cause trouble."

We live over close to the football stadium, and on Friday nights when the high school team has a home game, the streets can get crowded. Tonight they're playing North Sunflower, and even though it's an hour till game time, I have trouble getting into my own driveway. The nose of a Chevy van is sticking into one edge of the drive, and the rear end of a pickup truck's in the other edge. Somehow I manage to get between them without hitting either one.

Where we live and why we live here are matters of concern to Betty. We bought the house three years ago, right after I got the job managing the motel. Before that, we couldn't really afford to buy anything. I'd been working nights at a Mr. Quik, making just over minimum wage, and we'd been living off that and Betty's salary. She's a receptionist at the Southern Prime catfish plant.

The house isn't really a bad one, as houses go. Aside from the parking problem and the noise we have to put up with when there's a ball game, the property just has one or two quirky features. You can't see out of our bedroom because it doesn't have any windows. It's right in the middle of the house—our son's bedroom's on one side of us, the living room's on the other. Apparently, the lady that had the house built believed somebody was stalking her. She may have been right, because way back in 1969 somebody did come into the house one night and kill her. That's the other quirky feature, one we didn't find out about until a year ago, when Betty happened to notice it in the "25 Years Ago This Week" section of the *Enterprise-Tocsin*.

But mostly, what's wrong with our house is that it's not the kind of house Betty expected to live in when she married me. My dad owned a good portion of the farmland up in Coahoma County, and I grew up in a house that would hold seven or eight houses like this one. It's the house my brother lives in now.

Betty's in the kitchen, fixing supper for our son. Our sitter's a high school girl who's supposed to feed him and then take him to the game. We argued a little bit about whether or not we could afford to hire her. I said of course we could, and Betty said yes, of course, we can afford *any*thing.

I walk over to the stove and put my arms around her waist, encircling her from behind. "Hey," I say, "ready to go?"

"Almost."

She's wearing a new dress, the nice black one I gave her last Christmas. It's the first time I've seen her with it on. She looks good in it—the material's exactly the same color as her hair.

I kiss the back of her neck. She's damp there from the stove heat.

"I could eat not one but two or three cows," I say.

"Don't you dare," she says. "If you do, I'll take you to auction."

She's in a good mood, not worried about much, or if she's worried she's hiding it. Good times are still possible, I tell myself, and for a minute I've got an urge to walk across the street to the stadium, climb into the press box, and say it over the PA system: my wife and I are headed out to have fun, a good time's the only thing on our minds. As if announcing it would make it a fact of public record, like a stat in the Saturday sports pages.

Certain roads in Mississippi have become dangerous lately, in a way they never were before. Highway 82, which dips down into the Delta just west of Winona and streaks straight across it to Greenville, is one of the worst. Traffic has increased dramatically since the offshore casinos moved in, and on Friday and Saturday nights in particular, four lanes are not enough to handle all the craziness. Hill country gamblers come roaring down into the Delta with money to burn, and a few hours later they head home, broke and mad and drunk to boot. They generally run both the traffic lights in Indianola. Sometimes, just for the hell of it, they'll run you right off the road.

Right now we're headed west, the safer direction, but coming home we'll have to watch out. Coming home could be tricky.

"Any more trouble with the movie folks?" Betty says.

"Not today. But I imagine tonight, when they're all liquored up or drugged or whatever it is, they'll pitch a fit or two."

"I guess they just live for a wild time."

"I think most of them do. I kind of like Charles Rhett, though. He seems like a regular guy."

"Why?"

"I don't know. Seems like he's got his tormented side."

Something with a big engine in it's coming up behind us fast. In the glow of the car's headlights, Betty's face looks gray. "A tormented side," she says. "For you that's what makes somebody a regular guy? That's one hell of a note."

The other car whips past us, leaving us alone in the dark. Neither one of us says another word until we reach Greenville.

I drive on past all the fast-food places and chain restaurants that line 82—Bonanza zips by on the left, Western Sizzlin's on the right—and turn toward downtown.

"Where are we going?"

"You'll see."

Big houses—big *white* houses with Doric columns and verandas, houses that almost shout the word *Southern*—rise up on either side of Washington Avenue, the richest street in the Delta. At one time or another, I've been in most of these houses, but Betty's never been in any of them. What's inside, I want to tell her, is not all you imagine it to be. But you can't tell a person a thing like that. You can't even show them. Going inside and looking around for a few minutes or a few hours or even for a few days will only confirm what they already think.

We cross the railroad tracks. Straight ahead, a mile or so away, looms the levee. Above the levee, where the sky ought to be pitch black, there's a pinkish red glow. If you didn't know better, you might think Jesus had come again, but in fact it's just the Lady Luck Casino. The boat's docked at the Greenville wharf, and that pink glow's keeping folks at Mississippi Power and Light happy.

I turn right before we get to the levee. Just a block off Washington Avenue, the look of things changes. We pass a vacant lot, littered with bottles and cans and old tires. Across the street are little shotgun houses, with tin roofs and collapsed porches.

"You're not headed for Lee's?" Betty says. "Are you taking me to Lee's?"

This is the moment I've dreaded. For a second I feel like I'm an orange that's been on the juicer for a little too long. What's been squeezed out of me is spontaneity: the right to make an extravagant choice—even an extravagantly *bad* choice—and feel fine about it.

"You guessed it," I say.

"Are you out of your mind?"

"A little bit." I pull up in front of Lee's and cut the engine. "But it's my anniversary, and I must have been a little bit out of my mind when I married you."

For a second I can't believe I've said that. "What I mean," I tell her, "is that everybody's a little bit out of their mind, don't you think, when they fall in love?"

It's a small voice that comes back at me, the voice of a young girl. "I don't know, I can't remember what it felt like."

On these happy notes, we climb out of the car and trudge into the restaurant for the purpose of celebrating all our years together.

Lee's Eating Place is a clapboard shack in the bad part of town. The steps that lead to the porch are rickety, rotting. Next to the door, on a dangerous-looking bench, sits an old man, dressed like a porter, with a cap pulled down over his eyes. It looks like he's asleep.

The front room is the kitchen. Off to one side there's a big old potbellied stove where they bake the potatoes, and along the wall opposite there's a wide wooden counter where four women stand preparing the steaks and fixing salads. Another pair of women—the wait-resses—scurry around, picking up plates of steak and shrimp and hot tamales, pulling cans of beer from the big brown refrigerator in the corner.

The eating room—at Lee's there's no such thing as a dining room—is in the back. There are seven or eight long tables with red-and-white-checked tablecloths on them. Newspaper clippings decorate the walls. There's one from the Memphis paper, another from the Jackson paper and, right between those two, a long article from the New York Times. All of the articles praise Lee's. The one from the Times, which I remember reading ten or twelve years ago—the last time I was here—says Lee's serves the best steaks in the United States.

And at Lee's they respect their own reputation. The proof of this is their prices. A single steak costs almost forty dollars. That's one of the things everyone knows about Lee's, even those who haven't been here. It's also why Betty got pissed in the car.

But apparently she's decided to make the best of it. When the waitress comes, Betty smiles and asks to see a menu.

"We don't have menus," the waitress says. "We've got shrimp, tamales, spaghetti and steaks." She stands there waiting, the pad in one hand, a pen in the other.

Normally, this is when Betty bends over the menu, studying it, trying to decide what the best meal is for the money. But since there is no menu, she doesn't know what to do. She stares at the tablecloth, her dimple deepening as she considers the air. I begin to wish we weren't here. I want to reach across the table and take her hand and tell her that we can survive a dinner at Lee's, that ruin won't overtake us before we get home.

"We could share a steak," I say. "They're real big."

"Okay."

"A steak," I tell the waitress. "And two salads. And a couple of beers."

"Heineken or Bud?"

It's not fair to say that Betty kicks me, but her toe definitely makes contact with my shin. "Bud," I say. "Bud's fine."

The waitress leaves, and there we sit. It's still fairly early, there are only two other couples eating, and they're at tables on the far side of the room. Betty's eyes scan the walls, taking in the newspaper clippings. This is one of the places she's been hearing about her whole life. This is the kind of place she thought she'd be spending time at when she married me. She had every reason to expect a future that included dinners in restaurants that were not just a link in a chain, first-class air travel to places like Honolulu, his and hers Mercedes.

Why she didn't get that is still in some ways a puzzle, even to me. I know when she lost it, and I know how she lost it. It goes back to an evening about twelve years ago, when I was a junior in college. Betty and I had just gotten engaged, and my father had thrown a big dinner for us at the house. My brother and his wife were there. There were only the five of us—Momma had been dead for a couple of years—but Dad had hired a caterer anyway. Some wiry little chef from a fancy restaurant in Memphis came down and cooked fresh salmon—it had been flown in from someplace in the Northwest. The chef, who happened to be black, had three other black guys helping him, all of them dressed head to toe in white. I remember thinking there were almost as many cooks in the house as diners.

We were sitting at the dining room table, drinking espresso from cups so tiny you could hardly get enough of your finger through the handle to hold one of them. They'd brought out some sort of fruity dessert with cream on top of it. Dad waited until one of the black guys who was serving us left the room. Then he glanced over his shoulder, to make sure the door had closed. Seeing that it had, he leaned forward.

When a white Southerner does this after a black person leaves the room, it means *they* are about to be assessed and analyzed. Everybody else, as if by prior agreement, leans forward too. I did it myself that night.

"You notice how fast they're moving?" Dad said.

Everybody—including me—nodded. *They* were moving very fast.

"When they pulled up here today," Dad said, "and started unloading stuff out of their van, I noticed something real peculiar. One of 'em was climbing the stairs to the porch when he figured out he'd left a tray in the van. His hands were full of other stuff—trays and whatnot. So he turns around and hollers 'M. C., bring me that tray I left—it's over yonder behind the driver's seat.' And that damned M. C. or whatever his name is, he by God *ran* to the steps with that tray."

Dad tossed down his espresso. He held the cup by the rim, two-fingered. "I asked the chef, 'Pardon me, but I notice they're really working. How do you get 'em to do that?' He screws his face up and says, 'Well, they been working for me a long time. I try to treat 'em right, and they pretty much perform.'"

Dad looked around the table. He was fifty-five then, a big man with a reddish face that could turn dark blue when he got angry. When she was alive, Momma had always begged us not to upset him because one day, she said, he'd get so mad he'd have a stroke. That was exactly what happened, about a year after the night I'm describing.

"There's a lesson in all of this," Dad said. "You know what it is?"

I believe it was Betty who spoke, but I can't remember. Anyhow, somebody said, "What?"

"They'll work for one another," Dad said. "They won't work for a white man."

It helps to know that my relationship with Dad had never been easy. I had not been, as a kid, the kind of boy who likes to get in the pickup truck with his father and ride the turnrows, listening while the old man makes acute observations about soil conditions, the relative merits of different herbicides, or the advantages of hill-dropping a field. I'd never been interested in farming and did not ever expect to be.

I had not, for the past several years, been in agreement with my father about anything serious. I had voted for

Jimmy Carter. I had chosen to attend Ole Miss, rather than Mississippi State, and I was majoring in sociology, not agricultural economics like my older brother. The previous year, when Vice-President Bush came to Ole Miss to make a speech, Dad had seen me on the evening news, holding a sign that suggested certain links between the Reagan administration and Adolf Hitler. The next day he told me he wouldn't pay any more college tuition. A week or so later, he had a dream in which he saw my mother crying, and the image forced him to change his mind, though he warned me that I had two strikes against me.

Now, at his dinner table, a nasty curve was on the way. The twist was that I was both batter and pitcher.

"There's a lesson, all right," I said. "But you've missed it."

Normally, you think of color rising into a person's neck and spreading upward into his cheeks and ears when he gets mad. But on Dad the first feature to darken was his forehead. I swear, it turned navy blue.

"All right, Mr. Answer Man," he said. "Speak. What's the lesson?"

I was not and am not a religious person. But I prayed that when I spoke, my voice wouldn't crack. "The lesson," I said, "is that if you'll treat them right, they'll work. If you'll let them see some fruits of their labor."

"Would you like to see the fruits of your labor?" Dad said.

I didn't speak. Beside me, Betty somehow seemed smaller, as if she were falling in on herself. My brother sat across from me doing his best to conceal a smirk.

"There are no fruits," Dad said. "Because there's been no labor."

He got to his feet. He was wearing a suit that night, in honor of our engagement. He began to pace the room, his hands locked behind his back. "You're like those fellows in the kitchen there," he said, no longer bothering to keep his voice low. "You won't work for a white man."

He reviewed, primarily for Betty's benefit, the whole sorry history of my time on the planet. The first time I was sent to the field, he said, I had chopped down cotton and left everything else standing.

"The field hands told him," he said. "The *field hands* told my son how to tell a stalk of cotton from a cockle-bur, yet he persisted in chopping down the cotton."

Pulled from the field to save the family from ruin, I had been assigned the simple task of mowing the yard.

"Ran a new John Deere mower into the ditch and turned it over," Dad said. "Left it there overnight without saying a word to anybody, and we got a four-inch rain, and when we pulled that thing out of the ditch the next day, the engine was completely full of sludge."

He ran down the list of my transgressions, highlighting the truly heinous, weighting more heavily, it seemed, the more recent lapses in judgment and initiative.

When he had concluded, he came to stand behind his chair, his hands resting on the back of it. My brother and his wife sat staring into their laps. I couldn't bear to look at Betty.

But Dad could. He looked right at her. Slowly he shook his head. "Honey, you don't deserve this," he said.

The voice that came from beside me was surprisingly firm, determined. "I love him."

"Hell," Dad said, "so do I. But that don't mean I aim to give him one single penny for the rest of his life. What you give him, darling—well, that's up to you."

You could argue that he didn't mean it, that sooner or later he would have put me back into his will. But he took me out of it the next day, and he kept me out of it for a year, and then he died.

And now we're what we are.

What we are is two people who can't afford to be at a place like Lee's, who are meant to eat a smaller, cheaper piece of meat than the one the waitress brings to our table. She brings it on a big white platter. The steak looks like it's about an inch and a half thick.

They've made two or three surgical incisions in the meat, so that we can divide it up. I slice off a big piece for myself, and Betty cuts off a smaller one.

It literally melts in your mouth. We ordered ours medium, but the experience of eating it makes you think of rarity, of things that can't be done every day, that shouldn't be done every day, because then they'd lose their special nature.

"It's good," Betty says.

She reaches across the table then and takes my hand in hers. "I'm glad we came," she says. "I know it's crazy, but what the hell."

"We could do a lot of wild things," I tell her.

"Like what?"

She's smiling now, and for a second she looks like she's nineteen again, and I feel like I've just met her, on the steps of the Ole Miss union. It was snowing then. For all I know, it could be snowing now. The surroundings have faded away.

"We could slip out behind the gym and smoke."

"Jesus. You really mean it?"

"We could go climb the water tower behind the John Deere dealership."

"Wow."

"We could spray paint *Bob + Betty*—folks would see it from the highway."

"It gives me the shivers," she says, hugging herself, "just thinking about it."

At that moment, everybody in Lee's—the waitresses and cooks, the other couples and Betty, everybody but me, I guess—gets the shivers. The dining room quivers. Charles Rhett has just walked in.

"Goddam," he says. He waves a hand around the room. "This is real."

"It's real tacky," says the woman who's with him. Her hair is short and blonde, except that there's a purple streak right down the middle. It's hard to explain the thing that she's wearing. The best I can do is to say it's very tight, it's black, it's one piece, and from the distance of ten feet it looks like it's made out of rubber. If it's rubber, though, it's thin rubber. You can see the outline of her nipples.

"Let me guess," Rhett says to the waitress, whose hands dangle loosely at her sides while her mouth droops open wide. "Sit anywhere we want to, right?"

"Yes sir."

"What if we don't want to sit anywhere?" the blonde says.

The waitress says, "I'm sorry, ma'am?"

The blonde says, "Never mind."

Rhett puts his arm around the waitress. "That's right," he says. "Never mind. My friend here's just revealing her origins. She had the sad misfortune to grow up in Beverly Hills, where there was a shortage of role models. Nobody ever taught her how to behave because nobody out there knows."

They head for a table in the corner, underneath the *New York Times* piece. Betty watches them, her fork halted halfway to her mouth. I search her face for some sign of fascination, but I don't see any. If anything, there's a trace of distaste there. I know it wasn't caused by the steak.

I lift my beer can to sip from it. Maybe light glints off the aluminum, maybe Rhett just has keen peripheral vision—whatever the cause, he glances our way.

"Hey," he says. "Hey, Bob."

I start to choke on the beer. It's gone down the wrong way. I'm probably red in the face.

The next thing I know, they're standing beside our table, Charles Rhett and the blonde. "This is Libya," he says.

I have no idea what he's talking about. "What is?"

"This is," he says. His left hand closes around the back of the blonde's neck. He's hurting her—you can see it in her eyes, though she doesn't move or say a word. "That's her name. Y'all mind if we sit down?"

The waitress has followed them over. Rhett orders a steak and a beer. Libya asks the waitress if she's ever heard of a salad, and when the waitress says yes and starts to write on her pad, Libya says, "Wait a minute. I didn't say I wanted one."

The waitress looks as if she's about to cry. Maybe all her life, in some secret corner of herself, she's fantasized about being a movie star, about living in LA, going out from time to time to film things on location, visiting local restaurants and being admired. She's seen herself in that role again and again. Now, face to face with the real thing and finding that the real thing's made of rubber, she's lost something, she's not sure what.

"Just bring her a beer," Rhett says. "She draws sustenance from watching others eat. She likes to watch others do all sorts of things."

There's a strange gleam in his eye, and I can smell whiskey on his breath. He's still wearing the clothes he had on earlier, but he's got on a bunch of rings now, two on his right hand, two on his left. I don't know enough about gems to say what kind he's wearing, but they're big.

"Don't let us ruin your meal," he says. He looks at Betty and says, "Hell, I didn't introduce myself. I'm Charles Rhett."

Betty's fork travels to her mouth. She chews her meat and after she's swallowed it, she finally says, "I know."

"I like it here," Rhett says. "I like this place, I like this town, I like this state. I grew up in Tennessee. Sneedville."

Libya makes a face. "Jimmy Martin's hometown."

Betty says, "Who's Jimmy Martin?"

Libya says, "Who knows? Furthermore, who cares? But Sneedville's his hometown. I'm just telling you so Charles won't have to waste his breath."

"He's a bluegrass singer," I say.

Rhett reaches over and slaps me on my knee. "You like bluegrass?"

"Pretty well."

He sings a verse of "You Don't Know My Mind." Actually, he sings it pretty damn well. He sounds a lot like Jimmy Martin.

The waitress brings their beers. Rhett opens his and sucks about half of it down. Libya ignores hers.

Rhett stands his can on the table. He tells us his mother was a receptionist, that she used to work for the doctor who treated Jimmy Martin and all of Jimmy's kids.

"Jimmy's daughter was bad to get bronchitis," Rhett says. "Sometimes, in the afternoons, I'd be in the waiting room, waiting for Momma to get off work, when Jimmy brought the girl in. I never will forget that man, the way he acted toward me. This was right after he played on the *Circle* album with the Nitty Gritty Dirt Band. I mean he was somebody, but when I finally got up enough nerve to talk to him and he found out I loved his music, man, he really treated me well. I told him I messed around a little bit with the guitar, trying to play bluegrass, so the next time he came in and saw me sitting there, he pulled a pack of strings out of his pocket and handed them to me. It was a set of Martin Marquis. 'Try them,' he said. 'They're what I use.'"

"And so now," Libya says, popping the top on her beer, "Charles always tries to respond to the little man."

"What do you know about it?" Rhett says. His hand encircles the beer can now, his fingertips whiten. The can begins losing its perfect can-shape. Dents appear. "Some of us weren't born with a big house and everything we wanted. Some of us had to work to get it."

"Charles loves to cozy up to the little man," Libya says. "The little woman too. Charles remembers his roots."

The waitress brings Rhett his steak. He attacks it with his knife and fork, hacking off big chunks and eating them hard. Chewing, he makes a clicking noise. It sounds like the bones of his jaw are conflicted.

I finish as much of my steak as I want. Betty stopped eating a good while ago. To my surprise, she and Libya have started talking, and the conversation sounds pleasant enough.

"Your hair's pretty," Libya says. "It's soft and thick."

"Oh, it's just frumpy."

Libya runs her fingers through her own hair. "This stuff," she says, "it's so flyaway. You wouldn't believe what I've spent on it. But there's only so much money can do. In the end, your hair's your hair."

"I like the way you look," Betty says, and it occurs to me she really means it, that she might like to look the same way herself, running around in something that could pass for a scuba diving costume. It's strange to think your wife might be like that, and you never suspected it till now. She says, "You look—well, you look glamorous."

She sounds honest, not bitter. I wonder if she'll sound the same way later tonight, when we're at home alone.

"Well," I say, trying to catch Betty's eye, "think we should be going?"

"Hey," Rhett says, "what's your hurry?"

He's holding the fork with his right hand, but he's dropped his knife and grabbed my wrist with his left hand. He's squeezing it. It's not a pleasant sensation.

"We're headed for the Lady Luck," he says. "I'd like you all to be our guests."

The Lady Luck holds fast to the south side of the Greenville wharf. On the north side is the old Marina Restaurant. It was once a good cheap place to eat catfish, but now, I hear, the prices are sky-high, and the food's gone to hell. That's what happens when big money moves in.

Tonight the cobblestoned parking lot, which slopes down the levee to the water's edge, is covered up. You can see license plates from Arkansas, Tennessee, Louisiana, Texas. The air above is pink, as if somebody had shot it full of colored mist.

"Las Vegas on the levee," Rhett says. "It's good to see vice put to good use."

The governor says it's useful, that it generates revenue, and the legislature and a majority of the voters agree. But the truth is rents in Greenville and the other river towns have risen more than one hundred percent, and a lot of longtime residents have had to pack up. It's also true that the casinos have sparked a motel boom throughout the area, which is one of the reasons I've got my job.

Strolling down the levee, Libya hooks a heel in one of the cobblestones. She pitches forward and, upon landing, actually starts to roll.

"Goddam it," she hollers.

Having some experience in these matters, I lurch toward her, catch her by one leg, and stop her downward motion. For a second, she's on her back, staring up at me, and in that second I see a look on her face that I believe is gratitude. What I've done is probably all she needs anybody to do. I've just stopped her momentum.

The look vanishes fast. She's on her feet, pulling at one

elbow. There's a gash in the rubbery material. She skinned herself pretty bad.

"Son of a bitch," she says. She says it to me, as if somehow I'm responsible.

"At one time or another," I tell her, "every Delta girl of good character's taken a tumble on these cobblestones."

From behind I hear Betty's voice. "I never did."

"It's just a little thing," Rhett says.

He takes Betty's arm and leads her down the slope, leaving Libya and me to do the best we can.

When my dad was a young man, airplane travel was not a common thing. Like his father before him, like Delta planters all the way back to the end of the nineteenth century, he held two places dear. One was Memphis. It was sixty miles away, easily accessible, always available for what he referred to as a *little* big weekend." The other special place was New Orleans. It was reserved for the "*real* big weekend," two or three days of dusk-to-dawn drinking, punctuated—on those trips when Momma remained at home and he was accompanied by other men of his acquaintance—by visits to fancy brothels.

But for Delta planters of my era, those like my brother who have somehow managed to hang onto a large parcel of land, who are adept at milking the government's crop-subsidy programs, the weekend hot spot of choice is Las Vegas. They fly out of Memphis or Jackson on a Thursday afternoon, and when they return on Monday, booze oozing from their pores, they're worth several thousand less than they were worth when they left. I like to think that I wouldn't be going to Las Vegas, even if I had anything to go on. I like to think that, but I don't know for sure and won't know. Because long ago I did my gambling with my mouth. And lost big.

Offshore gambling is, among other things, an effort to bring Las Vegas to the planters. They might turn their noses up at the riverboat casinos, but they're here in force tonight. On the wharf, where a blues band is playing, I see several men from Indianola, cotton farmers who are also big in the catfish industry, as well as a couple of people from the north part of the Delta, guys I grew up with. If they recognize me, they don't let on. Neither do I.

The strange thing is, nobody seems to recognize Charles Rhett. We walk through the door, past a security guard who's there to keep out the underaged, and we're in a world of flash and clang, and everybody's mind is on something besides us. The waitresses are mostly naked, what little they've got on shines, but nobody pays them much attention either. They twist and swivel through the crowd, carrying drinks on trays. The drinks are free, but nobody seems to want one.

Everybody plays.

They play the slot machines. The slot-machine gamblers are mostly black, frequently female, though at one machine I see a grizzled white man who looks like he just climbed off a tractor—he's actually got red mud on his shoes. Every time he loses another dollar, he bangs his foot against the rail of his stool, and a gob of mud drops off.

They play blackjack. The blackjack players are all men, and they're wearing the sorts of clothes you'd expect to find on somebody like Porter Wagoner at the Grand Ole Opry. Loud colors, the countrified leisure-suit look.

Women hover nearby. One of them looks a little like Libya might look if she'd spent the day waiting tables out on 82.

"This is great," Rhett says. "This is fucking fabulous. A roomful of addicts channeling their addictions into revenue production."

He still has his arm around Betty. She continues to wear that look of distaste on her face—that little downward turn at the corners of her mouth—but she's not making any effort to pull away.

It surprises me when Rhett loops his other arm around my shoulder. He says, "Let's lose some money."

Betty says, "We've already lost it."

"You been here already?" Rhett says.

"No," Betty says. "We lost ours a long time ago."

"What my wife's trying to say," I tell Rhett, sliding out from under his arm, "is we can't afford to play."

"Can't afford to play?" Rhett says. "Hell, man, you can't afford not to."

I don't stop to think that he's merely saying what I've been saying for so long myself: that no matter how tight a vise you're in, you've still got to wiggle a little from time to time, even if it means that the screws just get tighter; one day you might up and wiggle free. I don't stop to think that my wife, despite the look she's maintaining, might enjoy walking around the casino and watching Charles Rhett throw money away, that she might enjoy a few minutes of glitz. I don't stop to think that it probably would be fun to play the slot machines or roll the dice, and I don't admit for even one second that neither of those activities, if indulged in moderation, would break me and Betty, any more than a steak dinner at Lee's did.

What I think is this: I started out above, and now I'm below. Charles Rhett started out down, and now, in a manner of speaking, he's up. I understand how I got where I am, and I can imagine how he got where he is. And for some reason, I know that if our roles were to be reversed right now—if I became the movie star and he became the manager of the Comfort Inn in Indianola, Mississippi—it wouldn't be any time before I'd crawl backwards into B-movies and daytime soaps and he'd become a corporate exec. For a second it seems pretty unfair.

"I'm going home," I say.

Libya says, "Will you take me back?"

"Sure," I say.

Rhett looks at Libya, and I look at my wife, and Betty's face never loses that faintly pissed-off expression, it never lights up as if to suggest she expects her luck to change.

It remains as it's been, quietly grim, even as she opens her mouth and says, "I'll stay."

In the parking lot, a car horn is blowing. It's on a silver Cadillac in the row facing ours. The car has Tennessee plates. The owner, a thin blond guy who's wearing a leather jacket and lots of gold chains and bracelets, is bent over under the hood pulling at something. His wife—or whoever she is—is sitting inside the car looking bored.

I unlock the passenger-side door of my car, and Libya gets in. "I don't have anything to lose by going home early," she says, staring straight ahead. "I hope you don't."

"I don't know if I do or not."

"Sometimes," she says, "you don't know till you've lost it."

"Sometimes," I say, "you can't tell even then."

I walk back to my side and get in.

The guy who owns the Cadillac jerks something lose under the hood and the horn quits blowing. He slams the hood and it starts again. He kicks the bumper then and goes around and releases the hood latch.

"Let's watch this," I say.

He bends over and jerks, and the horn stops, but when he slams the hood, it starts back. He runs this time—runs back to the door on the driver's side and pops the hood, runs back up front and jerks twice, and the horn quits blowing. This time, when he slams the hood, the horn stays quiet.

But when he gets into the car and shuts his door, the blowing starts again.

"Let's go," Libya says. "We may be witnessing a tragedy."

But for some reason I sit there transfixed. He jumps out of the car, lifts the hood and jerks twice, and the horn stops. This time he goes to the passenger side. He's really shaking. He opens the woman's door and says something to her. She gets out, and he gets in and slides across the seat, so that's he's behind the wheel. She gets back in then, and reaches for her door, and he looks over at her and starts to speak, but she's already grasped the handle. You can see his lips forming the word *no*. She shuts her door, and the horn begins to blow, and while we sit there watching, he clamps his hands around her neck and starts to choke her.

"Jesus Christ," Libya whispers. "Will you please start the goddam car?"

But all I can do is sit. I'm thinking that a mistake has been made. I'm thinking that somewhere in Michigan, somebody left something out, something that should have gone in, a component less essential than a crankcase, maybe, but something without which the Caddy can't be the car it was meant to become. It can only be the car that it is.

It's the car that it is, and the owner is the man that he is. It was his misfortune to buy this deficient car—if he'd bought a better car, he would be a better man. It was the misfortune of the woman he's choking to reach out and close that door. She's probably closed it a hundred times before, and nobody tried to choke her then.

I'll bet she's wishing she hadn't come here tonight. I'll bet she's cursing her luck.

Veneer

IT'S CALLED the Daily Planet. It's right next to the Tower Theatre, in a part of Fresno that everyone refers to as the Tower District. Most of the homes in this part of town are like mine: they were built in the teens and twenties, they fell into neglect in the fifties and sixties, then in the seventies and eighties, people like us, folks who either couldn't afford to buy in the north part of town or couldn't stand the thought of living in a house that looked just like the ones on both sides of it, moved in and refurbished.

The Planet is what I think of as an art deco sort of place. There's a lot of black-and-white tile, mirrors on the walls, some gilded metal here and there. Until tonight, whenever I've been here, there's been somebody parked behind the baby grand that stands adjacent to the bar. The pianist is always caressing standards, tunes like "Stardust" and "April in Paris." He's not here tonight because this is the Fourth of July, and most folks are in their backyards, cooking hot dogs or burgers and lining up the bottle rockets.

That's where I would be too except that my wife, Irena, and my daughters are in Prague, visiting Irena's family. In two more weeks I'll join them. But tonight I'm here with a friend.

The waiter seats us near the front of the restaurant, right next to the plate-glass window. Irena would never agree to sit here because we'd be visible from the street, and she fears a shooting. It's not an unreasonable fear. A few years ago an eighteen-year-old girl was killed on the sidewalk outside.

My friend, Emily, doesn't much like the location of our table either. "Aren't you afraid," she says, "that somebody'll drive by and see us sitting here and think we're having an affair?"

Emily has a certain reputation, and she stands what my dad, who spent most of his life raising cotton in the Mississippi Delta, would have called a strict-middling chance of attracting attention. She's got on bright purple skintight slacks and a black satin blouse against which her platinum hair sparkles.

"Let them think whatever they want to," I tell her. "We know we're not."

"You're not concerned with appearances, are you?"

"Just reality."

"At a certain point," she says, "the two become one."

I've known her a long time—I recognize the mood. Her father left her mother for another woman when she was seven, the same age as my twin daughters. For a long time her mother dragged her around California, chasing one man after another, getting poorer and drunker and needier.

Emily doesn't like holidays. She owns a lot of stock now in PG&E and runs her own home decorating business, but holidays make her feel like the outsider she used to be. On holidays she'll tell me that even though I grew up poor, I was always respectable. She'll tell me how easy I had it.

That's what she plans to do now. She takes a sip of Merlot and says, "What was the worst Fourth of July you ever endured?"

I try not to take her too seriously. If I take her too seriously, I could ruin a pleasant evening with one of my best friends. "All my Fourth of July's," I say, "were straight out of Norman Rockwell."

"They would be," she says.

I intend to change the subject, leave it at that.

I intend to, but then a waiter passes by carrying a plate. In the middle of the plate is a small strip steak, surrounded by substances that were never meant to come near it. It looks like there's mango sauce on that plate and something green. Mashed up kiwi fruit, maybe.

The steak reminds me of something, a story I could tell. Emily loves stories. She has the capacity to lose herself in a narrative. She and I go to suspense movies together—Irena only likes foreign films. At the climactic moments Emily clutches the back of the seat in front of her, gritting her teeth and perspiring. It's hard to pay attention to the movie once you've noticed that she's sitting there beside you taut and bathed in sweat.

The story I've thought of to tell her is one that we both might disappear into.

"Hey," I say, "wait a minute."

"What?"

"You want to hear a true story?"

"Where's it set?"

"Away down south in Dixie."

You can feel her mood starting to break. She tosses her hair, light from the fluorescent bulbs makes it shimmer. "What's it about?"

"The American Dream."

"On the Fourth of July? Jesus," she says. "Why not?"

The house I grew up in stood on sixteenth-section land in Sunflower County. It had started out as a tenant shack—just a couple of rooms, a tin roof, no running water. At some point before I was born, my dad and my grandfather, who died when I was still quite young, added indoor plumbing. That wasn't all they added. Every year or two, a room would be tacked on. For a while the house grew south, toward what we called "the main road," then it began to spread east, in the direction of Beaverdam Creek. The two original rooms were about a foot higher than all the others, except for the last room, the one closest to the creek—it was the highest of them all.

"Hope I don't ever need a wheelchair," Grandma said. "If I do, you just may as well shoot me."

The house featured porches on all four sides—if you could speak of anything so oddly shaped as having sides. At one time or another, three different rooms served as the kitchen. You could enter the bathroom from any one of three directions, a fact that caused my dad no end of anxiety. When he went in there, he'd spend several minutes locking all the doors, double- and triple-checking them.

My wife once said that my dad was a redneck Moses Herzog, and there's much in that description that is apt. Dad was a worried man. Like all farmers he worried about the weather, but his worries did not stop there.

Basically, I think, he worried because he couldn't figure out why he was what he was. He was a big tall man with a square chin and lots of wavy hair that would never go gray, and his blue eyes were in no way less bright or mischievous than those of Paul Newman. In the Navy he'd scored close to 160 on his IQ test. He'd read Tacitus in translation, he could quote vastly from *Paradise Lost*. Yet when he added everything up and summed himself, what he saw was a man with a small nondescript wife who slept in a separate bed and shrank at the touch of his hand. He saw a man who had little formal education, who hadn't even graduated from high school, a man who plowed the same furrows his own dad had plowed, who owed his soul to the Bank of Indianola.

He saw a man who lived in our house.

The house worried him. The other people who lived nearby on sixteenth-section land admired it, praising its size, the multiple porches, the unique configuration. ("It's shaped like the Panama Canal Zone," one neighbor said.) But the roof leaked, and the cypress tree on the east side kept sinking its roots into the septic pipes and backing up the toilet, and two or three times each spring Beaverdam Creek flooded—the water got into a couple of the rooms, and the floorboards rotted and had to be replaced.

The main thing wrong with our house, though, was

that it was unlike some of the other houses Dad had entered after he became a deacon at Beaverdam Baptist.

Beaverdam Baptist was a country church. For the most part the people who went there were folks like my family—small-time cotton farmers who'd soon be driven under by rising labor costs, the move toward mechanization, and the growing preference for synthetic fabrics—but quite a few rich people attended that church as well. The one my dad got to know best was another deacon, Tiny Bright.

Tiny was not his real name. His real name was Herbert. People called him Tiny because he weighed about 280 pounds. He owned five thousand acres of the best land in Sunflower County, and he also owned a cotton gin and was a partner in several businesses in Indianola. Most—though not all—of this wealth had been handed down to Tiny Bright by his father.

Despite his success, I've never believed that Tiny Bright was very smart. He once assured a girl of my acquaintance that the capital of Michigan was Milwaukee. Though he'd earned a degree at Mississippi State, his grammar was no better than Grandma's, and Grandma had left school after fifth grade. And things often exploded when he touched them. I once saw him try to air up a basketball at a church picnic—it blew up in his face. I once saw him try to air up the tire on his car, and it blew off the rim. No one else that I have ever known was inept enough to make a tire do that.

But Mr. Bright could do two things well. He could make money, and he could sing. He directed the choir at Beaverdam Baptist. He was a baritone who soloed exactly twenty-four times a year, at morning services on the first and third Sundays of each month. Attendance was always high then.

"When Tiny sings 'I come to the garden alone,'" Dad said, "everybody in the congregation wishes they could go to the garden with him."

We didn't go to the garden with Mr. Bright—or Brother Bright, as I called him then—but we did go to his house. We went to his house on June 28, 1970. I can date it so exactly because I had turned twelve the day before.

He invited us over for supper that Sunday after the evening service. He'd insisted we bring Grandma, so it was the four of us and Brother and Sister Bright, and their daughter, who was three or four at the time.

I don't remember too much about the evening. I do remember quite a bit about the house. It was perfectly symmetrical in every way, and it seemed to possess great mass. Also, there were thick white carpets on the floors, several bathrooms, each of which had only one entrance, and lots of gold-plated surfaces—on chandeliers, candlesticks, picture frames and lamps. A big grandfather clock stood in the corner of the dining room.

"Lovely," Dad kept saying at supper. "This is such a lovely evening, such a lovely home."

I had never heard him use the word *lovely* before. I had never heard anyone use that word before, and I don't think I've heard anyone use it since.

We had salad, baked potatoes, corn on the cob, and ribs, which Brother Bright cooked on a charcoal grill in his backyard. The grill lingered long in Dad's mind. It was probably the only object he saw that night that he could afford to buy.

"That's a fine way to fix meat," he said in the car on the

way home. "We're gonna get us one of those. Folks, we're gonna have a cookout on the Fourth of July."

People like Dad did not own grills.

They had never owned grills for the same reason that they could not countenance the idea of an animal—a dog or cat, I mean—living in the house. Animals belonged outside. If animals came inside, it diminished the distance between you—a creature who ought to have a roof over its head—and them. People like Dad, who had to submit bids on their land and their houses every five years, lived with the fear that one day they might not have a roof over their heads. To most people who occupied sixteenth-section land, cooking food outside would have seemed frivolous at best. Some would have said you were tempting fate.

I have often wondered what the grill meant to Dad. This is what I've come to think. I think that when he saw Tiny Bright cooking on the grill, his sense of possibility was altered. He understood that for a man like Tiny Bright, the whole world was home. And having understood that, he made a tremendous leap—a leap of faith. In the car on the way home, he must have decided that if you were willing to embrace Tiny Bright's vision—without knowing the sense of security all Tiny Brights knew—your world and his world might seem less far apart. You could bring a little breath of Tiny Bright into your life.

The Fourth of July fell on a Saturday. Friday afternoon, while Dad was out in the field plowing, Mother and

Grandma and I drove to town to buy the grill and various other supplies. Our first stop was the Western Auto.

There were four charcoal grills to choose from. Mr. Cecil Neil, who had run the Western Auto since the day it opened and who probably knew everyone in the south part of Sunflower County by name, extolled the virtues of each grill, so that by the time he'd finished, any rational person would have concluded that no differences existed between the most expensive grill—a big heavy-looking black thing like Tiny Bright's, with a wooden handle on the top and plastic wheels on the legs—and the cheapest grill, which was only four or five inches deep and made of very thin metal. You couldn't roll it from one place to another because the skimpy little legs lacked wheels.

The cheapest grill had been painted green. "You know what, Mr. Neil?" Mother said. "Seems to me like that little one there's the prettiest."

He was already pulling a flat white box off the shelf behind the display model. "A pretty grill," Mr. Neil said, winking at her, "for a pretty young lady."

Grandma had been busy on the other side of the store, over in the paint section. She met us at the cash register. She was carrying a pint can of latex enamel. From the patch on the label, you could tell that the paint inside was pink.

"I think I'll put a little veneer," she said, "on the coffee table."

I was in college before I had occasion to look up the word *veneer*. I can't remember what the occasion was, but it's probable that I had used the word in a strange way and been corrected by someone. Words frequently got me into trouble. When I was four or five, Mother had bought me a copy of *101 Dalmations*. Many of my happiest evenings were spent lying beside her, listening to her read it. She read it to me until the pages began to fall loose. Imagine my surprise when, in junior high, I learned from a girl I had a crush on that white dogs with black spots were not called Dallamontarians.

Those many years later, when I looked up the word *veneer*, my heart sank as I read down the list of definitions. Then I came to the last possibility, and after reading it, I dropped the dictionary on the floor and punched the air with my fist in a moment of pure triumph:

a superficial or deceptively attractive
appearance or display: GLOSS

"You think pink'll look all right on a coffee table?" Grandma asked Mr. Neil.

Mr. Neil said, "Pink will be fine."

Emily says, "You're telling me your grandmother painted the coffee table pink?"

We're on the salads now. The waiter brought them a few minutes ago. The waiter wore a long-sleeved pin-stripe shirt, black knee shorts, and a pair of tasseled loafers.

Our salads are potato crepes rolled in red lettuce leaves, sprinkled with shredded carrots and topped with guacamole.

"She did paint the coffee table pink," I say. "That very night. The evening of July 3, 1970."

"Why?"

"So it would look new for the Fourth of July."

"And this was something she did fairly often."

"She only painted the furniture a few times. Paint was expensive."

"But cheaper than new furniture."

"Cheaper and more colorful."

"And she liked color."

"She loved color. She loved color, and she loved junk. Once when we went to the Smoky Mountains—this was the only real vacation trip we ever took, by the way—she bought a bunch of chalk animals at a souvenir shop in Cherokee. A chalk dog, a chalk fox, a chalk hen and some chalk chicks. She stood them out in front of the house as decoration. It rained once or twice and they disintegrated. That's the sort of stuff she bought."

Emily lays her hand on my knee. A shiver runs up my thigh.

"So what happened on the Fourth of July?" she says. "What made it so bad?"

I don't exactly lay my hand on top of hers, but I do allow my fingertips to graze her thumb. "I'll tell you," I say, "if you prove you're woman enough to eat those crepes."

On the evening of July 3, 1970, we slept in a different house. It sounded like the same house—it was raining, and the rain beat down on the tin roof the same way it always had—but the odor of fresh paint, fresh *pink* paint, filled the air. The house smelled of chemicals, modernity.

Down the hall from my room, in the refrigerator, four T-bone steaks, pink also, lay on top of one another. They had been purchased in the afternoon at Piggly Wiggly. I had eaten steak before, of course, but I had never before eaten *a* steak. A steak was what professional football players always ate in my favorite books, the juvenile novels of the *Sports Illustrated* writer Tex Maule. Brad Thomas and Flash Werner and all the other members of Maule's fictitious LA Rams—they ate the very same thing that I would eat tomorrow. They sometimes ate it prepared the same way we would prepare ours—on a grill—and usually the grill stood on the balcony of an apartment overlooking the beach in a place like Santa Monica or Malibu.

Tomorrow would be almost like a trip to California. Flooded fields might lie just across the road, chicken droppings might litter the ground, and the closest body of water might be named Beaverdam Creek, but in my imagination I would stand near the Pacific, and while meat sizzled on the nearby grill, I would hear the mighty ocean roar.

"You'll take the steaks out," Dad told Mother, "and do whatever you do to a steak before it's cooked."

"Okay," she said.

"Me, I'll head on out back and start the grill," he said, "and then I've got to go down to the tractor shed and see if I can't figure out what's wrong with the John Deere. And Larry here, well, he's gonna be the chef for today."

Having explained everybody's role, Dad kissed Mother on the top of her head and mussed my hair and left the house.

"What do you do to a steak before you cook it?" I asked Mother.

"I don't know—I never have cooked one."

"Why didn't you say so?"

"That just wouldn't do."

"Why not?"

"Because that's not what your dad wants to hear."

He heard a lot of things he didn't want to hear from other people—bankers, implement dealers, insurance agents and the like—and I know he frequently heard one thing he didn't want to hear from Mother. *I'm tired, I don't really feel like it tonight.* She liked to give him good news whenever she could, so if it would make him feel better to think she knew how to prepare a T-bone steak, she was happy enough to say she did. Then maybe she wouldn't have to say yes to something else.

She dumped a lot of salt and pepper on the steaks, and then she decided to throw a little brown sugar on them too.

"That'll give 'em a little extra flavor," she said.

Grandma said, "If you ask me, them steaks was just a waste of money. For that price, you could have got a whole side of salt meat."

I said, "You can't cook salt meat on a grill."

The waiter comes to clear away our salad plates. I order another bottle of Pilsner Urquell. I ask him if this time he could put the bottle in the freezer for a few minutes before bringing it out. He looks at me with disdain. I feel almost as if he's seen the house I grew up in.

Emily says, "So your mother always said she was too tired?"

"Most of the time."

"How do you know?"

"The walls were thin, and I slept in the room next to theirs."

"Why didn't she want to make love?"

Why didn't she? I wonder. Why would anybody quit wanting to do that?

"She was a Southern Baptist," I tell Emily, knowing full well that I'm explaining nothing. "She'd already done what she was supposed to do—you're sitting across the table from the living proof of that."

"How did your dad feel about her?"

"He was mad about her."

"Just like you are," Emily says. "Mad about Irena, I mean."

There's an edge to her tone, as there always is when we're alone and my wife's name comes up. Emily has a tendency to think I'm undervalued. She'd be a lot more critical, I believe, if it weren't for my daughters. She says they're the greatest kids she's ever seen, that I'm a lucky man because I get to be their dad.

She says she's lucky because she gets to baby-sit them. One weekend last year, when she was taking care of them so we could go to a concert in San Francisco, we got home to find all three of them in the backyard, taking turns riding a Shetland pony. We were scared Emily had bought the pony for them, but it was only rented for one day.

"Just like I am," I agree. "He was mad about her—to all appearances, anyway. He only lived two weeks longer than she did. People said he grieved himself to death."

"I could see you doing that."

"Not too soon, I hope."

"Not too soon. But one day. Now tell me—what about the steaks?"

"The steaks?" I say. "Dad was mad about them too."

They must have been at least an inch thick. We'd bought the cheapest grill, but nobody could say we'd skimped on the steaks. When I stabbed the first one with a fork, it felt like it weighed a couple of pounds.

Beneath the grate the coals glowed red-hot. "How long does it take to cook a steak?" I asked Mother.

She was standing beside me holding the plate. "A long time," she said.

"How long?"

"Two or three hours, I imagine."

"It didn't take Mr. Bright that long to cook those ribs."

"Those were pork," she said. "This is *steak*."

She could hardly stand the thought of eating meat of any kind, she would have lived just fine off tomatoes and black-eyed peas. But the way her voice rose when she pronounced that weighty word—*steak*—assured me that even she was caught up in the spirit of our endeavor, that she held a certain truth to be self-evident: just like Tiny Bright, we were entitled to grill our meat, and on any given day our meat might be better than his.

I threw the first steak on the grate.

Mother said, "Hear that sucker sizzle."

She had never used the word *sucker* in that manner before. All of us, I felt, were pushing at our boundaries. We were reimagining ourselves. If you'd told me right then that I might one day see Pikes Peak, I would not have considered it impossible.

I threw another one on. "Two down," I said, "two to go."

"Pitch 'em on there," she said. "Get 'em hot."

In Tex Maule's novels, Brad Thomas was the LA Rams' quarterback. Brad came from Texas, a place every bit as much out of the way, I figured, as the place I was now. He'd made it all the way to LA, and so would I. I picked up my football and went out behind the barn.

For an hour or so I played an imaginary game against the hated San Francisco Forty-Niners. I bent down, barked signals, took the snap from center and dropped back. Chased from the pocket by panting linemen, I scrambled, dodging a section harrow that tried to trip me up. Over by the pump house, I cocked my arm and fired a bomb.

Once or twice the ball bounced into Dad's watermelon patch, and I had to tromp around in there hunting it, which always made me nervous because you never knew where a cottonmouth might be crawling. Each of those moments I treated as an official's time-out.

I imagined anxious fans in the LA Coliseum. *Come on, Brad,* I heard them yell, as I stepped gingerly among the melons, searching for the ball. *Hit Spider on a deep down and out. Come on, come on.*

"Come on!" It was Mother's voice. "Lord, Larry, look!"

I ran toward the barn. When I came around the corner, I saw smoke billowing up from the grill. Mother's hands were clamped to the sides of her head.

For a second I thought she was going to start tearing her hair out.

Grandma was standing there beside her. She shook her head. "People," she said, "wasn't meant to cook outside."

The steaks didn't look much like steaks anymore. They were very small. They were small, and they were black. After throwing water on them, we had to pry them off the grate. Part of each steak crumbled. Only the essence remained.

Which, as it turned out, was enough. When Dad came home from the tractor shed and saw how red Mother's eyes were, he said, "What's the matter?"

She said, "We burned the steaks."

Standing on the porch in his dirty khakis, with mud on his boots and an uncertain future, Dad made a decision. He decided to arrange his facial features in a smile. You could argue that it was the equivalent of pink paint on a rickety old table: utterly useless and oddly inappropriate. You could argue that it didn't fool anybody. But the truth is that it did fool someone: Dad himself. He felt that smile there, and he believed in what he felt, just as Grandma believed it when her eyes told her a pink coffee table was a beautiful thing.

"It's the Fourth of July," Dad said. "We planned to have a picnic.

He pulled Mother and me against his chest. He smelled of field dirt. And sweat.

He said, "I like my meat well done."

The Planet pot roast is supposed to be delicious, but the recollection of that meat I ate twenty-five years ago has robbed me of my appetite. Emily doesn't look too tempted either.

I look out the window. In the parking lot across the street, two white cops are talking to a young Hispanic guy whose hair is in a ponytail. He's wearing torn blue jeans, a stained T-shirt. The three of them are standing by a gleaming white Lexus. I know what's about to happen. They'll slap handcuffs on him, bend him over the hood. But just as I start to look away, so that I won't have to watch it, one of the cops puts his hand out. The guy in the T-shirt laughs and slaps the cop's palm, and then the cop laughs and says something, and the guy in the T-shirt unlocks the Lexus and climbs in.

"You ate the steaks?" Emily says.

"Every last bite," I tell her. "Every single one of us pretended it was the best meal we'd ever had. Even Mother ate hers. Later on, she went to the bathroom and got sick."

"That's awful."

"You asked me to tell you about my worst Fourth of July."

"Of course I did. So don't stop now."

"I've got to stop somewhere."

"You can't leave me hanging like that."

"What else do you want to know?"

"Everything."

"Like what?"

"Well, for instance, what about Tiny Bright?"

"What about him?"

"He was the catalyst—your dad wouldn't have bought the grill if it hadn't been for him. Right?"

"Right."

"So what happened to him?"

"Well," I say, "I can tell you if you really want to know."

"You say that like it ought to frighten me."

"If you want me to, I'll tie up all the loose ends. It's up to you."

"I'm game," she says.

So I tell her that the next year, in an effort to increase his cotton acreage without actually buying new land, Tiny Bright—Brother Bright—entered a bid on our portion of the sixteenth-section. I tell her that Brother Bright outbid Dad and that six months later we were living in a trailer out behind Weber's Truckstop, and the house that both Dad and I had grown up in, with all those tacked-on rooms, had mysteriously burned down. The only thing left standing was the chimney.

Her eyes start to fill now. She's probably thinking how my mother must have felt when she had to leave her home, how it must have hurt Dad to leave that house for the last time, to leave that land he'd worked all his life. She's probably wondering if Grandma got to take the pink table with her.

She's probably feeling compassion for the whole troubled world. And why not? It's a world where men run off after other women and leave their wives and little girls behind, where a young girl is murdered outside a tony restaurant. It's a world in which some people spend most of their lives being told no.

She's probably aching for all humankind. But those tear-filled eyes have focused on me.

Her hand squeezes my knee, and my hand squeezes her hand. I think of my own children, on the far side of the Atlantic, sleeping peacefully now in bed beside their mother, not knowing that back home in the New World, where it's still the Fourth of July and their dad has told a story about a dream gone awry, appearance and reality are about to converge.

Rottweiler

THIS HAPPENED back in the mid-eighties when I was living in the mountains near Blacksburg, Virginia, and coaching football at Virginia Tech. I was a first-year assistant, in charge of defensive ends. It was my first college coaching job, and though I didn't know it when all of this took place, it was going to be my last.

I was thirty-two at the time. I'd taken Wytheville High to the class A state championship the previous season. But that wasn't really why I got the job at Tech. I got it mostly because a guy I'd played with in college at William and Mary, Jack Davis, had been hired as head coach. Jack had brought me in late, after spring practice, because the first man he'd hired for the position hadn't worked out. He had wanted me, I can see now, because he thought I'd do a competent job and be easy to control. Those were the qualities most of the assistants on that staff shared—competence and a complete lack of imagination. We finished the season 2–9. At the end of the year, Jack fired several of us, and the next year he lost his own job.

But in August of 1985, I couldn't see what lay ahead, and I was not about to look back. If I had, I would have seen a string of winning seasons at a tiny high school, in a league that didn't matter, and a bunch of losing seasons at home. My marriage had fallen apart the previous summer, and the breakup had been bitter. I was looking for a new start. It seemed like I'd found it.

Most coaches won't conduct a full-scale practice on the Thursday before the first game of the season. They don't start doing stuff like that until they've lost a few games and gotten desperate and mad, and then when they do start doing it, they'll say it's because they're trying to toughen the team up and make them hungry. Really, though, it's punishment, and the effect is always the same. They get a bunch of people hurt, and they lose a few more games.

Jack started the punishment before there was any reason to—he was from the Woody Hays school, one of those guys who believed giving the team a water break was a sign of moral cowardice. He had them out there that Thursday afternoon, knocking heads and busting ass.

The scout team was running West Virginia's offense at the starting defense. On a sweep to our left, my best defensive end, a senior from Philadelphia who'd been picked for the preseason All-East team by *Street and Smith's Yearbook,* forgot to look outside to see if the split end was cracking back on him. Unfortunately he was.

This was back before they banned below-the-waist blocking on crackbacks. Normally a teammate won't go for another teammate's knee, but every day Jack reminded his players that this was not the Kingdom of Heaven, that in this world, the meek, the tenderhearted, would not thrive. The split end put his headgear right into my defensive end's knee. Even before he hit the ground, I knew it was serious.

He was a black kid from the inner city. He'd grown up tough, and in the few weeks I'd known him I'd never heard him complain, no matter how hard you ran him or how hard he got hit. But there he was, curled up on his side, clutching his knee, gritting his teeth and groaning.

"Shit," he hissed. "Coach, it hurts."

While the trainers bent over him, I walked over to the observation tower. Jack was up there, fifteen feet high, leaning on the railing, his whistle dangling from his neck. He had his sunglasses on, and he was chewing tobacco, and he looked tan and healthy and untroubled. Back then he was on the fast track. He'd been Danny Ford's offensive coordinator at Clemson when he was still in his twenties.

"You think we really need this extra scrimmage?" I said.

"There's nothing extra about it. It's a regular Thursday practice."

I knew better than to point or even nod toward the spot where the trainers and my defensive end were. I took a step closer to the tower, to make sure we were out of earshot.

"I've got a sophomore playing behind him," I said.

"Then let's get your sophomore on the field and get

him ready—looks like he'll be starting Saturday night. Remind him that on a sweep, the first thing he does is glance outside."

"Right," I said.

"Alex?"

I had turned toward the field. When I looked back up at Jack, he hadn't changed his position. He was still leaning on the railing.

"Some folks have a hard time making the transition from being the head coach to being an assistant. This is not Wytheville High."

"Right," I said.

That was all it was. I went back to practice, they carted my best player off to the hospital to rearrange his knee, and I made up my mind to forget about the encounter.

But later on, as I stood in the checkout line at Kroger, waiting to pay for a six-pack of beer and a deodorant stick, I thought about it again. I told myself Jack had been right. It was his show to run. I'd asked for input from my assistants, because that was my style. It wasn't his. If we got beat Saturday because a sophomore who'd never played a down of college ball froze up when they ran the option at him, I wouldn't have to answer the reporters' questions about it. He would.

What I didn't know right then was how quick Jack would be to shift the blame. "Obviously," he'd say, "our kid wasn't ready to make the right read. I imagine Coach Cahill will go over that with the defensive ends this week." Nothing would be said about the circumstances under which the player who should have been out there, the one who would have made the "right read," had gotten injured. Unlike my defensive end, Jack would always protect his flank.

When the checkout lady had rung up my stuff and told me how much I owed, she said, "And by the way, I think you and I are neighbors."

She was a tall heavy-breasted woman with long red hair and deep lines around the corners of her mouth. Late forties, early fifties. Her hands were rough, red-knuckled, and she spoke with a mountain twang. She didn't really look like she belonged in a store. She looked like she belonged outside, working the land. To the best of my knowledge I'd never seen her before.

"I live in the farmhouse down the road from you," she said.

"Which way?"

"Toward the boat dock."

"I haven't been down that way yet. I haven't had a chance yet to see much except the road between my place and town."

"I expect you've heard my son, though, haven't you?"

The truth was I had. I'd told Jack about it. The son, if that's what he was, had a voice that would have done any football coach proud. He could really bellow. I'd heard him at all hours of the night. There was a band of woods between the next house and mine, so I couldn't see much except the glow of a porch light, but I knew he was yelling at a dog.

Goddam you, he'd holler. *Get the fuck out of them roses.* Sometimes the dog barked back at him, but more often than not the son made all the noise.

"Yeah," I said, "I've heard him."

"He was in the military," she said, as if that explained it.

I pulled out a ten and handed it to her and told her my name.

"I'm June," she said, "June Mabus. You're a coach at Tech, aren't you?"

"That's right."

"Well, I'm a Tech fan."

"Wish us luck," I said, so she did, and then she handed me my change and bagged my beer.

It would be a while before I made a connection between my first meeting with June and what had happened that day at practice. Some time had to pass before I saw how many different things had started to end then, right when I thought everything was just beginning.

Football is a brutal game. But not everyone who plays it well is a brutal person.

I was all-state in high school in Murphy, North Carolina, and I started every game my last two years at William and Mary. I hurt a few people, though I never tried to—on occasion I got criticized by my own coaches for passing up a chance to drill somebody's quarterback after he'd let the ball go. What I tried to do instead was use my head and make all the right moves. As a defensive lineman, which is what I was, you can gain a split-second advantage by studying the offensive lineman's stance. Some guys put extra pressure on their fingertips on running plays, and that shows up around their nails. Some guys cock themselves if they're going to pull and trap, and others rock backwards on passing plays. Detecting all of that can be an art. If you're a good enough artist, you can make up for a lot of physical shortcomings. I tried to teach my players to use the brains God had given them, knowing full well that He'd been more generous with some in that regard than with others.

But that Saturday night, when we played West Virginia, it became apparent that He hadn't been unduly generous with any of our kids. We were down 14–0 at the end of the first quarter, 23–0 at the half. When it was all over, they'd whipped us 47–6. We scored our only touchdown with ten seconds remaining, and we scored it against their third-string defense and missed the extra point.

Afterwards, Jack closed the locker room to the media and cussed the kids for fifteen or twenty minutes, calling them names and shoveling out blame and promising them that come Monday afternoon, when most other teams around the country would be out in shorts and shoulder pads, they were going to beat one another black and blue.

"We're gonna find out," he said, "which dogs want to hunt and which ones want to hide in the kennel."

He stormed into the coaches' room then, and we followed him. In there he cussed several of the assistants. For whatever reason, he spared me, but I already knew that the season would be long and that at the end of it I might be gone. And right then I didn't think that would be such a horrible fate. By December, l figured, I might even welcome it.

I got home around midnight. I opened a beer and put George Jones on and turned out the lights and sat down on the couch. I knew better than to go to bed. I'd never been able to sleep after a ball game. It was one of the reasons my marriage had broken up.

My wife said it was freaky, the way I sat on the couch in the dark, win or lose, replaying the game. She would have found it even freakier if she'd known that I still remembered the score, quarter by quarter, of every game I'd ever coached in or played in, all the way back to junior high, as well as which end of the field my team had been defending. I remembered the good plays I or my players had made, as well as the bad ones, and I was fascinated, and troubled too, by the notion that the difference between a good play and a bad one was so often a matter of inches.

The game was unforgiving, but the severity of it was the very thing I loved. I had never played it perfectly, and I would never coach anyone else to play it perfectly, but at that time the attempt still seemed infinitely worthwhile.

I don't know how long I'd been sitting there in the dark going over the game before I became aware of the yelling. I got up and turned off the music and went outside.

I lived about ten miles from town. My house was on the side of a mountain, right across the New River from the Radford Arsenal. At that time the arsenal produced ninety-five percent of the U.S. Army's solid fuel. The next year, when I was living in Pennsylvania and selling life insurance, I'd pick up the Pittsburgh paper one morning and learn that a building at the arsenal had exploded, blowing everybody inside it to bits and damaging houses ten or twelve miles away. But that night it seemed like the explosion was taking place down the road at June Mabus's.

"You miserable bitch. You quit your whining. You don't got nobody to fuck you? Well, guess what. I don't got nobody to fuck me neither."

"Jimmy?" A woman's voice this time. "Honey, come on in."

I stepped away from the house and walked a little way into the woods. The porch light was on at June's house. Through the trees I could see a small guy and a large black dog. The guy, naked from the waist up, was kicking the dog. The dog shied away, carrying its hindquarters low the way an old stray will when you throw something at it. It was odd to see such a big dog doing that, especially when the guy was so little. I figured for a dog that big to put up with that, the fellow must have been kicking it ever since it was a puppy.

I went back inside. It was after two in the morning, but I knew I wasn't going to sleep any time soon, so I turned the lights on and decided to make myself a pot of coffee. I was sitting in the kitchen, drinking the first cup, wondering whether or not I ought to get involved, go ahead and call the ASPCA, when somebody knocked on the door. Somehow I knew it was June Mabus.

She had on a pair of faded jeans and a blue sweatshirt. There was sleep in her eyes, and her hair was tangled. She had some sort of plate in her hands. It was covered with tinfoil. "I saw your light on," she said.

"What's that you've got there?"

"Apple pie."

She pulled the tinfoil off to show me, like she thought

maybe I had my doubts. It wasn't a whole pie, just about two-thirds of one.

"Jimmy ate a piece or two," she said.

"Jimmy."

"My son."

"Sounds like he's got a problem with that dog of yours."

"I'm sorry about the yelling."

"He really ought not to kick that dog."

"No, he shouldn't. But he's going through a bad time—he's having trouble finding a job. The dog's in heat. She woke him up."

"She's about as big as he is, and I imagine she could be a lot meaner."

"She's not mean at all."

"What kind is she?"

"A Rottweiler."

"Damn."

"Look," June said, "I know it's crazy for me to show up like this, but I had to get out of the house." She offered me the pie. "Just take this, and I'll be going."

I realized then that I'd been blocking the doorway. "No," I said. "I can't sleep after a game. Come on in. We'll have some coffee." I led her into the dining room.

The house had been built right into the side of the mountain, and it had a big basement with a wood stove in it. The front of the house was level with the ground, but the back, where the dining room was, was about ten feet high. It felt like it was higher than that, though, because right beneath the window the hillside sloped dramatically, falling away toward the river, a thousand feet below.

On the far side of the river, at the arsenal, hundreds of tiny lights flickered. The arsenal kept three shifts going, working around the clock.

June nodded at the lights. "You know that's one of the Russians' top-ten targets?"

"The arsenal?"

"Ground zero."

"I guess one place is about as dangerous as another," I said. "If it ever comes to that, I mean."

"I guess so."

She drank her coffee. I wasn't hungry, but I ate a piece of the pie. It was good. She'd used fresh apples, and the crust tasted like she'd made it from scratch.

She told me she'd listened to the second half of the game on the radio. She hadn't gotten off work, she said, until eight, which was why she'd missed the first two quarters. She said that was the bad thing about working the afternoon shift: you missed all of the day games and half of the night games.

"Sounds like football's pretty important to you," I said. And then, without really thinking, I said, "You'd be the perfect wife for a coach."

"I was married to one," she said. "He's dead now."

"Where did he coach?"

"Everywhere." She said he'd been fired a lot. He'd started as an assistant at Salem High, teaching history and civics and physical education. "This was right after the Korean War," she said. "He thought he was lucky because he didn't have go back and work in the coal mines." When he got fired at Salem, she said, he got a job as an assistant at Floyd High, and after that he was an assistant at Pulaski High. "And after they fired him back in '63," she said, "nobody else offered him a coaching job. So he had to work in the coal mines anyway. He died in one ten years ago. A shaft collapsed."

It was a sad story. "These days," I said, "he probably wouldn't have been fired. Usually, when little high schools like those are losing, they just fire the head coach. The assistants keep their jobs. If they want them."

"He didn't get fired because the schools were losing," she said. "Everywhere he went, the teams won. He got fired because he beat me and he beat Jimmy, and he never was quiet about it. Believe me, those schools put up with it as long as they could. Because when it came to coaching football, he was damn good."

I like to think that if I had that night to live over, I'd remain silent at that point in the conversation, that as soon as it was decent to do so I'd put my hand to my mouth, as if I were trying to hide a yawn, and eventually June would get the message that it was time to go home. I like to think I wouldn't do again what I did then, because if I'd done something else, things might have turned out different.

What I did was pursue the subject. "I'm a pretty good coach too," I said. "But I sure was a piss-awful husband."

Like I said earlier, June had her share of wrinkles, and her hands were rough-looking. But when she stared at me across that dining room table at three A.M. and in a perfectly level voice said, "Did you hit your wife," I understood for the first time how beautiful a certain kind of hardness can be.

"No," I said, "but that doesn't mean I didn't beat her up."

It all spewed out of me, then, everything that had been

festering for more than a year, ever since the day I came
home from practice and found my wife gone. I told June
how I used to watch film until midnight, then go to bed
in my office and wake up and watch some more. During
the season, I ordered pizzas and ate at work, and then I
started doing it in the off-season too. I quit going anywhere with my wife, and when I went home and she
mentioned wanting to have a baby, I'd get right back in
the car and head for the office, where I'd switch on the
projector.

I told June that after a few years it didn't matter if my
team was winning or losing, I always reacted to the game
the same way. I was constantly searching for some way to
bridge the gap, so small and yet so vast, between a right
move and a wrong one.

"I never have been one of those guys who'll scream at
his players or hit them or kick them," I said, "but I've
known a lot of coaches who do—that's the kind of guy
Jack Davis is, if you want to be honest about it—and the
truth of it is, I'm not sure how different I am from them."

"Take my word for it," June said, "there's a big difference between somebody who smacks you and somebody
who doesn't."

"Ruthlessness is ruthlessness."

"You don't seem too ruthless to me."

"You're not married to me."

She reached across the table and took my hands in
hers. The contrast between her hands and mine was hard
to miss. Mine looked like they belonged on a woman,
and hers looked like they belonged on a miner.

She noticed the difference too. "You didn't do a lot of
offensive holding with these hands, did you?"

"I played strictly on defense."

"Are you playing defense now?"

I'm not going to say I hadn't thought about making love to her. What I am going to say is that when I realized I was thinking about it, it surprised me. It scared me a little bit too. I figured she was close to twenty years older than I was, and that crazy son of hers was just down the road, doing God knows what to a bitch in heat. But I hadn't been with anybody since my wife left me, and that was more than a year ago. And it felt good now to have June's hands holding mine.

I thought she might be shy about undressing, but she wasn't. "I like to be looked at," she said, standing by the side of my bed, pulling down her panties. "It's been a while since anybody did it."

She was actually quite nice to look at. Her breasts were big and full, and her thighs and hips were as smooth as her knuckles were rough. She crawled into bed beside me and put her hand between my legs.

"Looks like me and you," she said, "are in about the same shape."

We assumed several different shapes between then and the time we fell asleep. Both of us got wet, our bodies shiny beneath layers of sweat. Every time she came her teeth chattered, as if she were being raked by a blizzard. Afterwards, she made a lot of throaty noises, which I took for sounds of contentment. I don't think either of us ever said a word.

The sun was just coming up when we fell asleep. I woke up a short time later. The clock on the bedside table said 7:10 A.M. At first I couldn't imagine why I'd woken up so soon. Then I realized noises were coming from the basement. I stacked empty bottles and beer cans down there, to take them into town for recycling. I heard several of them tip over and roll across the floor.

The basement had three windows, all of which looked out over the river. There were two doors: one of them was at the foot of a flight of stairs that led to the living room, the other opened into the driveway. I felt sure I'd locked that door yesterday, before driving into town for the game.

I owned two guns, a pair of .22 target rifles my dad had left me when he died. I hadn't fired either of them in ten or twelve years. I kept them in the hall closet.

I crawled out of bed and pulled on my bathrobe and tiptoed into the hall. Whoever it was in the basement would sure as hell hear me moving around, and it was my fervent hope that just knowing I was up there and awake and on my feet would send the intruder running for the door. But I had a suspicion that he'd entered in the first place because he knew I was up there. I had a suspicion that June's crazy son was down in my basement, pissed off because I was with his mother.

I went to the closet and took out one of the rifles. I opened the bolt. The gun was loaded.

On the way down the stairs I heard another bottle go over. It never crossed my mind to wonder why, if it was June's son, he was making so much noise. From what I knew of him, he was the kind of fellow who had to make noise. Making noise, as far as I knew, was the thing he did best.

Holding the stock of the .22 with my right hand, I

grasped the doorknob with my left. I took a deep breath, turned the knob, and shoved the door open.

The dog was standing no more than three or four feet from me. She didn't flinch when the door opened. She stood her ground.

She was about waist-high, a big muscular Rottweiler that looked like she could take the leg off a man without working up a sweat.

The dog looked mean. She looked like a killer. She looked like an absolutely deadly animal, right up until the moment she whined and, stepping closer, tried her best to nuzzle at the folds of my robe.

After West Virginia mopped the floor with us, we had two easy games. We played both VMI and Richmond in Blacksburg, and we beat up on them. The only conclusion anybody should have drawn from those games was that we'd hammered two teams that didn't belong in division one. But for Jack, it was confirmation that the rough road was the right road. We kept scrimmaging four days a week, we put the down linemen through one-on-one drills every day, and the defensive ends and linebackers endured what Jack called the "box drill": it required the defensive player to crouch in a three-by-three-foot square and meet the charge of an offensive lineman who'd had a twenty-yard running start. The most common form of injury this caused was a rotator cuff strain, which is what ends a lot of major league pitching careers. It's not as serious an injury for most football players, though. You just shoot cortisone into their shoulders a few hours before the game, and they can still throw a forearm in the other guy's face. But the folks our guys would be throwing them against were going to get a lot bigger and a lot stronger. We had Miami coming up. Down there, in the Orange Bowl.

I was less and less interested in what happened on the football field. I'd begun to wonder if I was cut out to coach at this level—or, for that matter, at any level. There was something Jack and several of the others had, an urge to succeed no matter what the cost, that it looked like I lacked. I worried quite a bit about the cost.

What went on at home was a lot more pleasant.

June had started coming by my place every evening. She usually brought the Rottweiler with her. The dog's name was Dottie, and she liked to lie down in one particular spot, right under the dining room window, and fall asleep. She'd lie there and not make a sound, unless she had a bad dream, and then she'd start to whimper, and June or I would go and wake her up.

Most nights June brought food with her too. She picked up fried chicken sometimes when she was leaving the grocery store, but more often than not she brought the makings along and cooked in my kitchen.

"They claim this is the best way to find a man's heart, don't they?" she said.

"Are you prospecting?"

I hadn't intended the question seriously, but that was how she took it. She was standing near the stove when I asked it, a big pot of stew starting to boil on the eye. She turned the flame down, then wiped her hands on her apron.

"No," she said. "I like to eat and I like to screw, and I like to do them both with you. But I don't expect to get to do them with you forever. I figure when we teed it up, we were already in the fourth quarter."

"How'd you arrive at that determination?"

"I got out my driver's license," she said, "and I looked there where it says *date of birth*. And I figured out the difference between that date and the day we met. Fifty-one years, one month, and several days."

She didn't have much formal education, but she had a lot of sense. When we were making love, I sure wasn't thinking about the difference in her age and mine, about those rough hands and her Clinch Mountain twang, and I wasn't thinking about them when I shoveled all that good home-cooked food down my throat. But at other times I did think about them.

We hadn't gone out together a single time. I hadn't asked her to any of the games, either, and I got two free tickets to each of them. I could rationalize and tell myself she had to work, but she could have gotten off. I'm ashamed to admit it, but I hadn't invited her because my free tickets were for seats in the same section of the stadium as all the other coaches' were, and I knew I'd have to weather a bunch of snide comments if June sat near their wives and girlfriends.

"You're young at heart," I said.

She swiped a few strands of hair off her forehead. "Yeah, I guess you could say I am," she said. "Or you could just as easy say my heart's about as old as the New River, and they say the New River may be the oldest river in the world."

I got up from the table and walked over and stood behind her and put my arms around her. I rested my chin on top of her head. Her hair smelled like she'd just washed it. I don't know what kind of shampoo she used, but every now and then I catch a whiff of it in some woman's hair, and for a minute or two I'm back there, my arms around June, the two of us standing just a few feet away from a thousand-foot drop, nothing but air and a river between us and something so explosive it could blow Moscow right off the map.

"Jimmy knows I've been stopping by here," she said.

"Yeah? What about it?"

"I don't think he likes it."

"That's too bad," I said. "Does it worry you?"

"No. I just thought I'd mention it."

"Okay," I said.

I began kissing the side of her neck, then, and rubbing her breasts, and in no time we'd forgotten about Jimmy.

Or at least I had. But the next afternoon, right before I drove into town and boarded the team bus to Roanoke, where we'd catch our flight to Miami, I remembered him. I didn't have any choice. Because Jimmy called attention to himself.

I had packed my bag and put it in the car and gone back inside to make sure I'd turned off the coffee maker when I heard a sharp crack. The first report was followed by six more in quick succession. Somebody had just emptied a clip. The noise had come from the direction of the woods that hid June's house from mine.

I opened the front door and ran outside. He was standing with his back against a tree, closer to my house than theirs. He'd just jammed another clip in.

He was wearing olive green fatigues. He also had on a

pair of boots that looked like they belonged on a trooper. He wore his hair in a crew cut.

He glanced at me. Then he raised the pistol and pointed it at the trunk of a tall live oak that stood about fifty feet away, right where the land sloped down toward the river.

This time he'd inserted a double clip. He fired fifteen shots, one after another. He was quite a marksman. Every single shot hit the tree. The bullets knocked off big chunks of bark.

After he quit firing, the other sound registered. I realized then that I'd been hearing it for some time. Maybe since he first started shooting.

I looked past him, through the woods, in the direction of June's. I couldn't see too much of the house, but I knew the dog was inside. Her wailing sounded muffled.

I imagined her in there, nose pressed against the pane, her paws on the windowsill, nails scratching at the paint, wet tongue dangling out one side of her mouth. She knew something wasn't right. But all she knew to do about it was stand there and watch and make noise.

The noise made by sixty thousand people, jammed elbow to elbow into the Orange Bowl on a warm October evening, was scary. It made you think of the Nazis, of those party day rallies in Nuremburg.

"We're fixing to shut them up," Jack hollered at me on the sideline.

He had his headset on. His face was bright red. He always worked himself up before a game, and when he was just about the same hue as an August sunset, he barged into the locker room and addressed the team. I'd heard him say the wildest things before games, stuff that would have generated national headlines if the media ever got wind of it.

Tonight he'd told them that a friend of his, a high school coach from New Jersey who was in a position to verify facts, had found out that Miami's quarterback, a junior all-American from Trenton, had been caught exposing himself to little girls when he went home last summer. It had all been hushed up, Jack said, but it was the truth, and sooner or later it was going to come out. "You intend to let a guy like that," he yelled, "complete a pass against you? How in the hell could you live down the shame?"

They won the toss and returned the kick to their own 23. They lined up for the first play in a single back set, with two wide receivers in a slot to their left. It was a set we'd seen on the films. So far this season, when they were in it, they'd either run behind the left side of the line or flooded the zones on that side, going most often to the receiver underneath. On pass plays the tight end always set up to block, then released into the right flat. They hadn't thrown to him a single time.

The coverage we'd devised for this set worried me. We were going to rotate the left corner into a deep zone and ask our left tackle to take an outside rush for containment. The defensive end would play like a linebacker, covering the tight end, if he released, man to man.

This was the same kid who'd replaced the one whose knee had been torn up. He'd had a tough time even against the teams we'd been playing the last couple of weeks. He'd been learning to read the option, and now we were asking him to play pass defense.

The tight end set up to block, then slid into the flat. And instead of going with him, our kid froze for just an instant, then barreled headlong toward the quarterback.

"Cover!" I hollered.

Exhibitionist or not, their quarterback read the coverage perfectly. He looked for his safety valve, saw the tight end wide open, and lofted a pass into the flat.

There was nothing between the receiver and our goal line but seventy yards of grass and a 180-pound cornerback. Our guy was game, but Miami's tight end weighed 260 pounds. He ran right over the corner. He went into the end zone high-stepping, the ball held aloft.

I was still watching him when somebody grabbed my elbow and spun me around.

Jack had already made the classic gesture, tearing off his headset. Now it looked like he aimed to tear off my head. His face was about an inch from mine—I swear I could see a strand of roast beef trapped between his front teeth.

"We practiced that the whole fucking week," he said. He grabbed the front of my shirt.

Jack had been a tailback in college. When we were players, I had probably outweighed him by fifty pounds, and now, even though he had a potbelly, I imagine I still had a good thirty-five- to forty-pound advantage. I didn't want to use it there on the sideline in front of sixty thousand fans and our whole team, but I didn't want his hands on me either.

"Let go of me," I said.

"What?"

"Let go of me."

He looked down at his hands. Gradually he loosened his grip.

"You're too passive," he said. "If you'd done that to me, I would have tried to kill you."

"That's the difference," I said, "between you and me."

It was not a small difference, and it was not the only difference. And as I stood there on the sideline, watching Miami shred our defense and feeling oddly uninvolved, I understood that the game I'd devoted so much of my life to was made for the likes of Jack and not for the likes of me. It had its fine points, its subtleties, and it wasn't always the most physically talented team that came out on top. But it almost always was.

In the end, brute strength, speed, and sheer meanness would win. On the football field, those meant everything. Even if they weren't much use anywhere else.

I don't know for sure what time I got home. It was probably around three A.M. On the flight back to Roanoke, Jack and I hadn't spoken, and when our bus reached Blacksburg, I had walked straight to my car. If he thought he could achieve anything by yelling at everybody, if he believed that could somehow wipe out a 42-point differential, he was welcome to do it. I didn't plan to listen to any more hollering that night.

When I got home, I went straight to bed. For the first time in my life, I felt no urge to replay the game. I put my head on the pillow and fell dead asleep.

What woke me was the dog. For a minute or two I lay

there listening to her barking. It sounded different this time. At first I couldn't quite figure out what was different about it. Then I realized that dog was close by.

I got out of bed, walked over to the window and looked out. It must have been around five-thirty or six. The sky was light gray, but you couldn't see much because a fog had settled in, blanketing the mountainside.

I raised the sash. It sounded as if the Rottweiler was in that band of woods between my house and June's. Once I thought I saw her, a dark shape moving about among the trees, but I wasn't sure then, and I'm not sure now.

She kept the barking up. I say barking, but coming from her it sounded whiny. It sounded as if she was feeling pain, rather than getting ready to inflict it.

I thought about going out there and calling to her, but I rejected the idea. Likely as not Jimmy was inside the house, throwing a fit, and I didn't see what I could do about it. I didn't want to go down the hill and find him screaming at June, see her standing there taking it. I didn't want to get shot, I didn't even want to risk a fistfight. I lowered the window and went back to bed and laid the pillow on top of my head.

I woke up the next time a little after ten A.M. By then the fog had cleared. The day was cool and bright.

When I went out to the road to get Saturday's mail, I saw all the vehicles clustered near June's mailbox. There were three or four cars from the Montgomery County sheriff's department down there, as well as an ambulance. The ambulance just stood there. Its lights weren't flashing.

I remained where I was, my hand on the latch of my

mailbox. I scanned the road and the woods, trying to see if the dog was out, moving around, as if her presence would tell me anything. It was several seconds before I realized that the deputies, when they got there and saw that dog, would have shot her with a stun gun.

They wouldn't have risked letting her bite them. They didn't know how hopelessly docile that Rottweiler was.

Bohemia

WHEN JANIE wakes, Richard is standing naked near the sink, brushing his teeth. The train is moving slowly now, bouncing over the rails. It's light out, she can see gray patches through the rift between the curtains.

"They need to do a little maintenance on these tracks," Richard says. "Even if all those Nazis hadn't come through here, you could tell we'd crossed the Czech border. It's just like when you cross into Mississippi on I-55. You know you've come to raggedy-ass place."

The raggedy-ass place they're bound for is Prague. The Nazis Richard has just referred to weren't real Nazis, they were German and Czech border officials.

They gave Richard a rough time. They ransacked his bags, they pulled the covers off his bunk, they opened his guitar case and took the guitar out and shook it. After he playfully called one of the Germans "Adolf," they strip-searched him.

He fits the profile, Janie knows, of a drug smuggler. He's in his mid-twenties, he's American, he's got wild-looking hair. And beyond all that, his behavior suggests he loves to put one over on folks that have authority.

She wipes sleep from her eyes. "How much longer?"

"It's 8:15. We're supposed to be there at 9:20."

He lays his toothbrush down and turns around. He's wearing his glasses, with those bottle-thick lenses. He almost never takes them off. Two years ago he was in a car wreck, and he suffered severe optic nerve damage. His eyesight grows worse and worse. Before too long, he'll go blind. That's why they're traveling. He wants to see some sights while he still has eyes to see with.

Right now he's a sight to see. He's got a huge erection. Janie begins to tingle in all her secret places, all those tucked-away spots that Richard knows so well.

He grins at her. "Just as hard," he says, "as an old bow-wow's bone."

They're about to ring up another nation. So far they've rung up France, Belgium, Switzerland and Germany. In the few months she's known Richard their borders have been constantly expanding. First they rang up counties, beginning with those closest to Jackson, then they rang up all the nearby states—Louisiana, Alabama, Tennessee, Arkansas. Then Janie's aunt died and left her the money, and they began to ring up countries.

It's Richard who keeps track of the places they ring up. When they're doing it, she doesn't know where she is. Or care.

She throws the blanket off, and as she looks the length of herself, at the high rising breasts and the swell that is her belly, at her big knees that are parting now to receive Richard, she marvels once more that either of them can love her body. Yet both of them do.

"We've got time," Richard whispers as he crawls into the bunk. His nose nestles in the valley between her neck and shoulder. "Sweetheart, we've got time."

And money, he says, too.

Because they've got money, they take a taxi from the railway station to a hotel. Capitalism has brought higher prices to the Czech Republic, but their pocket guide says the hotel they're headed for is a charming nineteenth-century establishment, with good service and reasonable rates.

On the way over Richard says, "I hope it's not too run-down. We're in that part of the world now."

Richard has told her he grew up in a two-bedroom house in west Jackson. The shutters on the windows didn't work, the roof leaked, and from time to time sewage backed up and made the toilet overflow. Richard knows run-down when he sees it, and on this trip he intends to avoid it.

But nothing Janie sees from the taxi seems the slightest bit run-down. The streets are clean, and most of the buildings look freshly painted, with intricate scrollwork around windows and doorways. Flowerpots adorn almost every windowsill. There's a lot of pink in Prague. The pinkness makes her feel light.

The sign over the hotel is pink neon. *Splendid,* it says.

That's the name of the place—the Hotel Splendid. The sign isn't lit now, but you can imagine how it will look at night. There are big dips and swirls in all the letters, especially the *S*.

"Let's stay," Richard says. He gestures at the street,

which is only a block long. This seems to be a residential area. "There's not shit going on here right now," he says, "but I bet you things rev up after dark."

Inside, at the desk, they hand over their passports. Behind the desk clerk there's a glass-fronted refrigerator filled with Czech beer and Pepsi Cola. Big bottles of beer cost twenty crowns—eighty cents—and the soft drinks are fifteen. The taxi just took them halfway across town for two dollars.

"A little money's going to go a long way here," Richard whispers in her ear, "and we've got a lot more than a little."

While the clerk copies the numbers off their passports, they look around the lobby. It has a high ceiling, dingy beige walls; on the floor, a burgundy carpet. There are no chairs or tables, no international papers like there were at all the places they stayed in western Europe.

Directly across from the desk, there's the entrance to the lounge. The sign says it opens at eleven.

A woman is waiting there. She's wearing a tight pair of black jeans and a bright red blouse. She glances at her watch, as if she's impatient. She's about thirty, a blonde, tall and tan. She has the kind of slim-hipped grace that Janie hates in a woman but loves in a man.

Sometimes she dreams she's losing Richard to a tall slim woman. The woman never has a face—Janie always sees her from behind. In the dreams, when Richard leaves her, the woman waits impatiently across the lobby of a train station or an airport. Richard pats Janie on the head or kisses her on the cheek. He tells her he never meant any of the things he said about loving her body, they were all lies. He says he was broke and she had

access to money, and he hopes he gave good value for the
dollar. He says he wishes she'd forgive him someday, but
she says she never will. What she means is she'll never
forgive him for telling her the truth.

She looks at him now to see if he's interested in the
woman who's wearing the red blouse. He doesn't seem to
be. He's craning his neck and squinting, trying to see the
prices of the items in the refrigerated display case. He's
never done anything to make her have those dreams. She
promises herself that the next time she starts to have one,
she's going to wake up. She's going to sit up in bed and
open her eyes.

The clerk's English is flawless. "How do you wish to
pay for the room?"

Janie pulls the Visa from her purse. A gold card is the
kind of thing she can have now. She owns a house in
north Jackson, an eight-year-old Jaguar, a piece of rich
Delta farmland she's never laid eyes on.

About all she doesn't have is a plan for the future. Like
Richard, she's afflicted by limited vision. She isn't looking
beyond the room that's waiting upstairs, beyond the bed
she knows she'll find there.

That's the problem a lot of people have had with her:
she lives in the moment, and her moments are intense.
Her mother gave up on her when she was still a kid. Janie
threw tantrums because they ate supper at five-fifteen,
right in the middle of her favorite TV show, so that her
dad could get to work at the warehouse by six. Her dad
said he didn't enjoy much of anything except food and
sleep, and she was ruining half his pleasure. Every few
nights he pulled her pants down and spanked her in
front of her brother. Finally her mother told her she

could carry a tray to her room and eat before the set. Janie kept the practice up. She still does it. Only now she eats before the TV set with Richard, and thanks to her aunt, the set is in a room about as big as her mother's house.

In the elevator she and Richard stand side by side—there's barely space for them and their bags and the guitar case.

"I could be wrong," Richard says, "so don't hold me to it." He pauses then as he always does before he tells her something important. "But you know what, baby?"

"What?"

"I'm starting to get a sneaking feeling that Prague may be our kind of place."

She doesn't ask him why. She knows it's because in Prague, so much can be had for so little.

She first met Richard in the snack bar out at the community college in Raymond. She'd just moved in with her aunt. Part of their deal was that she had to go to school.

She tried to make the best of it. She liked art appreciation, and her drama class was okay too, but she had trouble with history and English. She'd never been able to read very fast. Sometimes she had to read a sentence four or five times before she understood what the writer was saying. After it took her twenty minutes to get through a page, she didn't think too much of herself. She'd sit in the snack bar, eating sweets and drinking coffee, trying to work up enough energy to attempt another page. She was doing that when Richard walked over to her table and asked if he could sit down.

Her mouth was full. She was eating a chocolate donut, and something told her she had brown smudges on her face. She reached up and made a couple of swipes. Somehow she managed not to look and see if there were stains on her hand.

It was November at the time and cold at night. Richard was wearing a thin yellow windbreaker. It looked as if he had a T-shirt on underneath. He wasn't carrying any books. He wasn't carrying anything at all.

He said, "I'll come right to the point."

He told her his name was Richard Kinny. He said he was twenty-three years old, unemployed, with no prospects. He said he had grown up in Jackson, then gone away to Boston to study at the Berklee College of Music. In Boston, he confessed, he'd let his life fall apart. He'd done drugs, had a bad car wreck, damaged his eyes to the point where he could no longer read musical notation. A year ago he was living on the street. Now he stayed with his uncle, who was a janitor here at the college.

He said he had a thing for Janie. He'd been watching her—he'd seen her in here almost every night. One evening about a month or so ago, he'd been sitting at the table next to hers when she dropped her pen on the floor. She might not remember any of this, he told her, but she'd had on a loose-fitting blouse, and when she leaned over to pick up her pen he got an eyeful.

He couldn't quit thinking about it. If she wanted to call campus security because of what he'd just told her, she could go right ahead.

She said, "You've got nerve."

"I figure one day, hopefully not too soon, I'll be dead. I

don't want to leave this world without saying what's on my mind. Tonight seemed like the time."

She wasn't somebody who'd fall for just any line. She knew a thing or two about guys, because for most of her life they had treated her as if she were one of them. In high school and then later on, when she was working as a waitress down on the coast, her friends had been males.

Before moving in with her aunt, she'd shared an apartment with three members of a Biloxi rock band. At night, after they finished shaking the walls at whatever little joint had hired them, they came home and shook the walls some more. It was a rare evening when they didn't manage to pick up two or three women, many of whom would have made good lead vocalists: night after night she lay in bed listening to a litany of high-pitched shrieks, sounds so extreme in character that they seemed to come from someplace beyond the boundaries of human experience.

In the morning, the band members would parade into her bedroom to praise or complain. *This* one had gotten sloppy afterwards, *that* one turned out to be frigid. The *other* one was an earthquake and a tornado, all rolled into one.

But here was something new. Richard might make a fool of her, but if he did, at least she could say she hadn't made a fool of herself.

"My name's Janie," she told him. She asked if he wanted to go for a ride.

In the parking lot, he walked straight to her aunt's red Jag. When she asked him how he knew which car she drove, he said, "I may have shitty eyesight, but I sure pay attention."

He could find his way around Hinds County; he directed her on back roads until they located a nice parking spot near the edge of a pasture. There he proved he could find his way around her; his hands were under her blouse before she shut off the engine.

He said, "Bet I know where *your* ignition keys are."

She felt hot breath on her neck. The fingers of a maestro played her nipples.

Her aunt was already sick then; she'd been sick even before Janie moved in. She was letting an herbalist treat her for stomach cancer. All you had to do was look at her, and you could see the treatment wasn't working.

She didn't want to make a spectacle of herself in the end, she said. She did not intend to die in a hospital bed, with lots of tubes stuck in her nose. When it happened it would happen at home.

Except for Janie, she was alone. She'd married a rich doctor who'd left her ten years ago for a younger woman. When she moved in, Janie had known that agreeing to attend school was only part of the bargain. The other part was that she had to be willing to watch her aunt die.

What she hadn't counted on was having Richard around to help. Those last few weeks she needed all the help she could get. Her aunt threw up, wet the bed, soiled her nightgown.

"I'm firing from both ends," she said.

Richard would lift her from the bed, while Janie held her breath, gnawed her lip and stripped off the sheets.

"Don't worry, aunt," he'd say. "I've seen worse than this."

"I don't believe you."

"Would I lie to you?"

"Richard," her aunt said, "intuition tells me that you'd lie to anybody if need be."

Richard is not a big man, but in his arms her aunt looked like a shriveled-up doll. He leaned over and kissed her forehead. "I don't feel the need," he said, "to lie to you."

Her last few smiles were spent on him. "Is that true?"

"Right now it is."

"So where have you seen worse than this?"

"Up north."

"Tell me about it."

"It wouldn't be uplifting."

"I'm about to experience the biggest uplift of all."

"How about I sing you a song?"

"A song," she said, "is probably just what I need."

"Anything special?"

"Something from the sixties."

So Janie put fresh sheets on, and they got her aunt cleaned up, and then Richard perched on the edge of the bed, his guitar on his knee, and sang her a lot of old stuff by Dylan and the Byrds and the Beatles.

He was the one who walked in and found her dead. "She appreciated good lyrics," he said.

Their room at the Splendid is on the third floor, directly above the hotel's outdoor café. It's smaller than some of the rooms they've slept in lately, but she likes the windows. They start about three feet from the floor and reach almost to the ceiling. "Isn't this nice and airy?" she says.

"Yeah," Richard says, "but come see this."

He shows her there are two bathrooms. One of them contains the tub and a washbasin; the other, which is hardly big enough to stand in, has the toilet.

"Look." He sits down on the toilet seat. The wall is so close his knees rub against it. "Are Czechs little people?"

"I don't think so."

"I may have to alter my technique if I need to take a dump here."

He leaves aside any suggestion the toilet space may be too small for her, but she believes that's what he's got on his mind. She loves him for not saying it, for introducing her to the situation and letting her decide.

"If it gets too tight," she says, "we can just shit in the tub."

That starts them both laughing, and as always when they're happy they end up in bed.

They lie around the room for a while, making love and snorting coke. Richard carries their supply in his guitar. He's showed her the thick piece of wood inside the sound box—he says the piece is called the block—where the neck of the guitar joins the body. The block is glued on; Richard pries it off. There's a hollow steel tube inside the neck. The tube is full of plastic sandwich bags, and each of the bags contains several grams of coke. It's just for recreation, he's not selling on this trip. He hopes he'll never have to sell again.

About one or two he starts to get bored. There's no television set in the room, and he can't play his guitar now because he's glued the block back on and laid the instrument in the case to let the glue dry.

Janie could lie around naked forever, but when she

sees Richard growing restless, walking over to the window two or three times to look out, prowling the room like a caged cat, she knows it's time to put on her clothes. She's wary of overexposure.

"You want to go somewhere?"

He's in his underwear, a pair of black silk ones she bought him. "Sure."

He sounds ecstatic. He sounds as if it's the most wonderful thing in the world, the thought that they might go somewhere. This strikes her as odd. They've been traveling for six weeks. They haven't slept in any one bed for more than three nights. If there's one thing they've been doing, it's going.

She gets the guidebook out. The map on the inside cover is tiny, with only the major streets labeled. She finds Wenceslas Square, Hradĉany Castle, Mala Strana. What she can't find is any mention of the street they're on now. She hates the thought of asking someone for directions. It's not her lack of languages that inhibits her, she's not afraid to point or squeeze her legs together to indicate that she needs a place to pee. But when you ask for directions, you depend on another, which is something she'd rather not do. She'd rather pay for what she gets, and thanks to her aunt she's able to.

She says, "Let's take a taxi."

The taxi lets them out on Wenceslas Square. It's not really a square, it's a long rectangle, with a broad median. One-way traffic moves down each side. The air smells of diesel.

At one end of the rectangle, in front of a building the guidebook says is the National Museum, there's a huge statue of a guy on horseback. The rider is Wenceslas, a king the Czechs used to have back when they had a kingdom.

Shops and cafes line the sidewalks, and there are people everywhere, thousands of them. It's summer, the town is full of tourists.

"Wow," Richard says. "Is this Europe or what?"

"This is Europe," she says, almost as if she's the proprietor.

Crossing to the median, she takes his hand. Crowds and traffic make her feel protective of him. His peripheral vision is all but gone. He might get run over. He might lose sight of her or she of him, and where would they be if that happened?

They walk slowly toward the statue. Near the base of it, according to the guidebook, a famous incident took place. In 1968, after the Russians invaded, a student carried a can of gasoline into Wenceslas Square and doused himself in fuel. While hundreds watched, he struck a match and burst into flames.

A crowd has gathered there now. She assumes there's some sort of memorial at the foot of the statue, something she can't see for all the bodies. But then a gap opens up, and the spectacle is before her.

A skinny man, naked but for a pair of cutoff blue jeans, holds a silver sword. He waves the sword for all to see. Then he reaches down and picks up an aerosol can. Whatever is in the can he sprays on the sword.

The man sets the can down. He grips the blade right where it meets the hilt. He tips his head back.

A woman hides her face in her hands.

The man begins to feed himself the sword. Inch by

gleaming inch it disappears, until all you can see is the handle.

Expressions of amazement: she hears German, English—"Son of a bitch!"—French, possibly Italian, though for all she knows it could just as well be Fanti. Spectators toss notes and coins into a cardboard box.

Richard says, "Let's give the guy a buck. He's got a good routine."

But her hand won't move toward her purse. She stands motionless, watching the man, wondering what it feels like to swallow so much steel. She wonders if that cold blade burns going down, wonders if it sears his esophagus.

Nobody threw money at the student when he set himself on fire. She's a little hazy on the history of the Eastern Bloc, but she knows the student burned himself up for a reason. He was a man with convictions, one who acted on principles. It seems wrong to her, profane even, that this is now the site of an act that belongs in the circus.

Late afternoon: from the bank of the Vltava they achieve a perfect view of Hradĉany Castle. It stands on top of a hill, big and white, walled and impregnable. At night the castle is supposed to be a shocking sight.

"I'd hate to try to storm that bastard," Richard says.

"Did somebody try to?"

"Sure. Somebody always tries to storm a castle. Just like I stormed you."

"You didn't have to work too hard."

"The hell I didn't. I lay in wait for days, marshaling my forces and mustering my courage. Then I advanced across the plains—which in our case was the floor of the snack bar."

"And I gave in right away."

"You did not. I could hear the machinery working in your brain. It sounded like metal on metal, all those gears and wheels grinding. You were thinking *Is this guy for real or what?*"

It troubles Janie for him to know that. It smacks of calculation, and calculation is not something she likes to think of when she thinks about herself and Richard. You can't think of calculation and not think about numbers and the way they pile up.

They advance along a narrow cobblestoned street into the heart of Old Town. There's a big square here. In the middle of the square stands the old town hall, which has a famous clock on one outside wall. The clock dates back four or five hundred years.

Right across from the town hall is the building where Franz Kafka used to live. The ground floor is now a museum. Because Richard wants to, they go in and look around. The museum doesn't display a lot of articles, just a few photographs and drawings of the guy and the original covers of a few of his books. She's never heard of him until now.

Richard says Kafka was one weird dude, that he was engaged to the same woman for close to ten years, though he only saw her twice. He didn't believe he was worthy of her, Richard says, but he never could quite let her go.

He starts telling her about a story Kafka wrote, one in which a character wakes up to discover he's turned into a giant cockroach. It's all about alienation, he says, about feeling like you're not quite human.

She's had that feeling a few times herself. The day, for instance, when she walked into her room and found her brother and three of his friends stretching her bra out and measuring the distance from end to end. Or the time she and one of the musicians she used to live with were sitting on her bed smoking dope and he asked her if she'd take off her clothes and let him look at her because he'd never seen a big woman naked. Another time, her father happened to be driving by Baskin Robbins when she walked out with a three-tiered cone. He must have been drunk—he slammed on his brakes, right in the middle of Highland Drive. "Hey, Big 'un," he hollered, "you want a ride home?"

She doesn't need a dead writer to tell her about feeling less than human. And she doesn't need Richard to tell her that it's a hot day and they've walked a long way and it might be nice to sit down and have a drink. But he does.

They take seats under a big white umbrella with the Pilsner Urquell emblem on it, and when the waitress comes, they order two beers.

"It's supposed to be the best beer in the world," Richard says.

It's good: cold and bitter, with a yeasty aftertaste.

Richard locks his hands behind his head. He leans back in his chair. "Isn't this the life?"

"This is the life."

"I had my doubts about coming here, but this place is all right. Everybody's having a good time. I bet you there's one hell of a nightlife."

In the *Prague Post,* an English-language newspaper she picked up at the train station, it says Czechs earn, on the average, under three hundred dollars a month. She wonders how far that will go.

She wonders, for the first time, how far what she has will go. The answer isn't hard to arrive at. Sooner or later, it's going to run out. It may be two years, it may be three or four, but it won't be twenty. It won't even be ten. She's going to be what she was. Or something worse.

She says, "It's okay for a few days. I don't think I'd want to stay here much longer."

"I think I could hang around here forever."

"What would you do?"

"Do?" he says. The eyes behind those thick lenses look empty now, puzzled. "I'd do what I'm doing."

She almost says *Which is?* Instead she says, "I mean what would you do to make money?"

As soon as the sentence is out of her mouth, she wishes she could get it back. It's a perfect opportunity for him to repeat his last statement: *I'd do what I'm doing.*

He picks up his beer glass. He studies the yellow liquid. He might be a brewmaster looking for some visible clue, something that could tell what goes into such a heavenly brew.

"I'd become a professional faster," he says. "I'd take up a position back there on Wenceslas Square, close to where that guy was eating the sword, and I'd see how long I could go without food. I'd be getting tips for my performance and at the same time cutting my expenses."

She waits for him to say that she might try that too. She waits for him to cut her core to pieces, like that blade would if the sword swallower hiccuped. She waits for the words that will burn her heart up.

She waits, but the words don't come. "You know what?" he says.

"What?"

Reaching across the table, he takes her hand in his. He says he's a worthless sort, so she may want to disregard his opinion, but it seems to him that she'd look nice across the river in the castle, way up there on the hill. He says she ought to wear a crown and wield a scepter, have a thousand knights kneeling at the base of her throne, making royal fools of themselves, working hard to win her favor.

He tells her she's a princess: the Princess of Prague.

They fall asleep early, around ten o'clock. It's the first time that's happened on the whole trip. They've drunk a lot and eaten a lot and walked more than either of them is used to.

She has the dream again. Richard is saying goodbye. The dream starts out near the check-in desk at the airport in Jackson. This time the tall slim woman is absent, but Janie knows she's waiting for him somewhere. He's got his guitar and a backpack, and he's bare-chested. He isn't wearing anything except his underwear—he doesn't even wear shoes.

I'm going, he says.

Where?

Prague.

Why there?

Because, he says, *it's a place where a man like me can make a living.*

She asks him what he'll do there, and he says he's got a new routine. *Watch this,* he says.

He sets down the guitar case and opens it and takes out the guitar. He grabs the neck of the guitar, raises the instrument into the air, and throws back his head. His mouth opens wide.

She grabs him. *What are you doing?*

He says he aims to eat it.

She asks him why, and he says *For practice.*

He says that's how he'll make his way from now on, he'll be a full-service entertainer, he'll play and he'll sing, and then he'll eat his instrument, he'll offer music and freakery and tragedy, all for one price. Something for everyone, good value on the dollar, a better show than you'll see at the circus.

When she wakes, he's gone. At first she thinks she's still in the dream. Then she sits up in bed and lays her hand on her thigh. Her body is here, and she's never argued with the physical evidence that her body represents. So she prepares herself. Everything that follows *will* be real.

Naked, she climbs out of bed, runs her hand along the wall until she feels the light switch, and flips it on. She turns toward the corner where his guitar case should be. She knows it will be gone.

She knows it will be gone, and so will his bags. The only thing he'll leave behind will be those glasses. She'll find them on the table, beside her ransacked purse. When she picks the glasses up and sets them on the bridge of her nose—something she should have done long before now—she'll discover that the lenses have no refracting powers, that he's seen her with his own eyes, just as she is.

And in that moment, it will bother her that she's naked. It will bother her so much she'll become immobile. Her brain will say *move,* but her limbs won't obey. It will be as if something thick and hard were restraining them, as if she were suddenly encased in a shell, a creature of nightmare.

These are the thoughts she's thinking. She thinks them even as she sees the familiar guitar case, the suitcases beside it, as she feels his arms encircling her stomach, his fingertips creeping toward her breasts, reaching for her nipples, the cool hard surface of his lenses as he nuzzles the nape of her neck.

"I had to answer the call of nature," he says, and she agrees nature is impossible to ignore.

The Rest of Her Life

THE DOG was a mixture of God knows how many breeds, but the vet had told them he was at least part German shepherd. You could see it in his shoulders, and you could hear it when he barked, which he was doing that night in 1977 when they pulled up at the gate and Chuckie cut the engine.

"Butch is out," Dee Ann said. "That's kind of strange."

Chuckie didn't say anything. He'd looked across the yard and seen her momma's car in the driveway, and he was disappointed. Dee Ann's momma had told her earlier that she was going to buy some garden supplies at Western Auto and then eat something at the Sonic, and she'd said if she got back home and unloaded her purchases in time, she might run over to Greenville with one of her friends from work and watch a movie. Dee Ann had relayed the news to Chuckie tonight when he picked her up from work. That had gotten his hopes up.

The last two Saturday nights her momma had gone to Greenville, and they'd made love on the couch. They'd done it before in the car, but Chuckie said it was a lot nicer when you did it in the house. As far as she was concerned, the major difference was that they stood a much greater chance of getting caught. If her momma had walked in on them, she would not have gone crazy and ordered Chuckie away, she would have stayed calm and sat down and warned them not to do something that could hurt them later on. "There're things y'all can do now," she would have said, "that can mess y'all's lives up bad."

Dee Ann leaned across the seat and kissed Chuckie. "You don't smell *too* much like a Budweiser brewery," she said. "Want to come in with me?"

"Sure. "

Butch was waiting at the gate, whimpering, his front paws up on the railing. Dee Ann released the latch, and they went in and walked across the yard, the dog trotting along behind them.

The front door was locked—a fact that Chuckie corroborated the next day. She knocked, but even though both the living room and the kitchen were lit up, her momma didn't come. Dee Ann waited a few seconds, then rummaged through her purse and found the key. It didn't occur to her that somebody might have come home with her momma, that they might be back in the bedroom together, doing what she and Chuckie had done. Her momma still believed that if she could tough it out a few more months, Dee Ann's daddy would recover his senses and come back. Most of his belongings were still here.

Dee Ann unlocked the door and pushed it open. Crossing the threshold, she looked back over her shoulder at

Chuckie. His eyes were shut. They didn't stay shut for long, he was probably just blinking, but that instant in which she saw them closed was enough to frighten her. She quickly looked into the living room. Everything was as it should be: the black leather couch stood against the far wall, the glass coffee table in front of it, two armchairs pulled up to the table at forty-five-degree angles. The paper lay on the mantelpiece, right where her momma always left it.

"Momma?" she called. "It's me and Chuckie."

As she waited for a reply, the dog rushed past her. He darted into the kitchen. Again they heard him whimper.

She made an effort to follow the dog, but Chuckie laid his hand on her shoulder. "Wait a minute," he said. Afterwards he could never explain to anyone's satisfaction, least of all his own, why he had restrained her.

Earlier that evening, as she stood behind the checkout counter at the grocery store where she was working that summer, she had seen her daddy. He was standing on the sidewalk, looking in through the thick plate-glass window, grinning at her.

It was late, and as always on Saturday evening, downtown Loring was virtually deserted. If people wanted to shop or go someplace to eat, they'd be out on the highway, at the Sonic or the new Pizza Hut. If they had enough money, they'd just head for Greenville. It had been a long time since anything much went on downtown after dark, which made her daddy's presence here that much more unusual. He waved, then walked over to the door.

The manager was in back, totaling the day's receipts. Except for him and Dee Ann and one stock boy who was over in the dairy aisle sweeping up, the store was empty.

Her daddy wore a pair of khaki pants and a short-sleeved pullover with an alligator on the pocket. He had on his funny-looking leather cap that reminded her of the ones policemen wore. He liked to wear that cap when he was out driving the MG.

"Hey, sweets," he said.

Even with the counter between them, she could smell whiskey on his breath. He had that strange light in his eyes.

"Hi, Daddy."

"When'd you start working nights?"

"A couple of weeks back."

"Don't get in the way of you and Buckie, does it?"

She started to correct him, tell him her boyfriend's name was Chuckie, but then she thought *Why bother?* He'd always been the kind of father who couldn't remember how old she was or what grade she was in. Sometimes he had trouble remembering she existed: years ago he'd brought her to this same grocery store, and after buying some food for his hunting dog, he'd forgotten about her and left her sitting on the floor in front of the magazine rack. The store manager had taken her home.

"Working nights is okay," she said. "My boyfriend'll be picking me up in a few minutes."

"Got a big night planned?"

"We'll probably just ride around a little bit and then head on home."

Her daddy reached into his pocket and pulled out his wallet. He extracted a twenty and handed it to her.

"Here," he said. "You kids do something fun. On me. See a movie or get yourselves a six-pack of Dr. Pepper."

He laughed, to show her he wasn't serious about the Dr. Pepper, and then he stepped around the end of the counter and kissed her cheek. "You're still the greatest little girl in the world," he said, "even if you're not very little anymore."

He was holding her close. In addition to whiskey, she could smell aftershave and deodorant and something else—a faint trace of perfume. She hadn't seen the MG on the street, but it was probably parked in the lot outside, and she bet his girlfriend was in it. She was just three years older than Dee Ann, a junior up at Delta State, though people said she wasn't going to school anymore. She and Dee Ann's daddy were living together in an apartment near the flower shop he used to own and run. He'd sold the shop last fall, just before he left home.

He didn't work anymore, and Dee Ann's momma had said she didn't know how he aimed to live, once the money from his business was gone. The other thing she didn't know—because nobody had told her—was that folks said his girlfriend sold drugs. Folks said he might be involved in that too.

He pecked her on the cheek once more, told her to have a good time with her boyfriend and to tell her momma he said hello, and then he walked out the door. Just as he left, the manager hit the switch, and the aisle lights went off.

That last detail—the lights going off when he walked out of the store—must have been significant, because the

next day, as Dee Ann sat on the couch at her grandmother's house, knee to knee with the Loring County
sheriff, Jim Wheeler, it kept coming up.

"You're sure about that?" Wheeler said for the third or
fourth time. "When your daddy left the grocery store, Mr.
Lindsey was just turning out the lights?"

Her grandmother was in bed down the hall. The doctor and two women from the Methodist church were with
her. She'd been having chest pains off and on all day.

The dining room table was covered with food people
had brought: two hams, a roast, a fried chicken, dish
upon dish of potato salad, coleslaw, baked beans, two or
three pecan pies, a pound cake. By the time the sheriff
came, Chuckie had been there twice already—once in the
morning with his momma and again in the afternoon
with his daddy—and both times he had eaten. While his
mother sat on the couch with Dee Ann, sniffling and
holding her hand, and his father admired the knick-
knacks on the mantelpiece, Chuckie had parked himself
at the dining room table and begun devouring one slice
of pie after another, occasionally glancing through the
doorway at Dee Ann. The distance between where he was
and where she was could not be measured by any known
means. She knew it, and he did, but he apparently believed that if he kept his mouth full, they wouldn't have
to acknowledge it yet.

"Yes, sir," she told the sheriff. "He'd just left when Mr.
Lindsey turned off the lights."

A pocket-sized notebook lay open on Wheeler's knee.
He held a ballpoint pen with his stubby fingers. He didn't
know it yet, but he was going to get a lot of criticism for
what he did in the next few days. Some people would say

it cost him reelection. "And what time does Mr. Lindsey generally turn off the lights on a Saturday night?"

"Right around eight o'clock."

"And was that when he did it last night?"

"Yes, sir."

"You're sure about that?"

"Yes, sir."

"Well, that's what Mr. Lindsey says too," Wheeler said. He closed the notebook and put it in his shirt pocket. "Course, being as he was in the back of the store, he didn't actually see you talking with your daddy."

"No," she said. "You can't see the checkout counter from back there."

Wheeler stood, and she did, too. To her surprise, he pulled her close to him. He was a compact man, not much taller than she was.

She felt his warm breath on her cheek. "I sure am sorry about all of this, honey," he said. "But don't you worry. I guarantee you I'll get to the bottom of it. Even if it kills me."

Even if it kills me.

She remembers that phrase in those rare instances when she sees Jim Wheeler on the street downtown. He's an old man now, in his early sixties, white-haired and potbellied. For years he's worked at the catfish processing plant, though nobody seems to know what he does. Most people can tell you what he doesn't do. He's not responsible for security—he doesn't carry a gun. He's not front-office. He's not a foreman or a shift supervisor, and he has nothing to do with the live-haul trucks.

Chuckie works for Delta Electric, and once a month he goes to the plant to service the generators. He says Wheeler is always outside, wandering around, his head down, his feet scarcely rising off the pavement. Sometimes he talks to himself.

"I was out there last week," Chuckie told her not long ago, "and I'd just gone through the front gates, and there he was. He was off to my right, walking along the fence, carrying this bucket."

"What kind of bucket?"

"Looked like maybe it had some kind of caulking mix in it—there was this thick white stuff sticking to the sides. Anyway, he was shuffling along there, and he was talking to beat the band."

"What was he saying?"

They were at the breakfast table when they had this conversation. Their daughter Cynthia was finishing a bowl of cereal and staring into an algebra textbook. Chuckie glanced toward Cynthia, rolled his eyes at Dee Ann, then looked down at the table. He lifted his coffee cup, drained it, and left for work.

But that night, when he crawled into bed beside her and switched off the light, she brought it up again. "I want to know what Jim Wheeler was saying to himself," she said, "when you saw him last week."

They weren't touching—they always left plenty of space between them—but she could tell he'd gone rigid. He did his best to sound groggy. "Nothing much."

She was rigid now too, lying stiffly on her back, staring

up into the dark. "Nothing much is not nothing. Nothing much is still something."

"Won't you ever let it go?"

"*You* brought his name up. You bring his name up, then you get this reaction from me, and then you're mad."

He rolled onto his side. He was looking at her, but she knew he couldn't make out her features. He wouldn't lay his palm on her cheek, wouldn't trace her jawbone like he used to. "Yeah, I brought his name up," he said. "I bring his name up, if you've noticed, about once a year. I bring his name up, and I bring up Lou Pierce's name, and I'd bring up Barry Lancaster's name, too, if he hadn't had the good fortune to move on to bigger things than being DA in a ten-cent Delta town. I keep hoping I'll bring one of their names up, and after I say it, it'll be like I just said John Doe or Cecil Poe or Theodore G. Bilbo. I keep hoping I'll say it and you'll just let it go."

The ceiling fan, which was turned off, had begun to take shape. It looked like a big dark bird, frozen in midswoop. Three or four times she had woken up near dawn and seen that shape there, and it was all she could do to keep from screaming. One time she stuck her fist in her mouth and bit her knuckle.

"What was he saying?"

"He was talking to a quarterback."

"What?"

"He was talking to a quarterback. He was saying some kind of crap like 'Hit Jimmy over the middle.' He probably walks around all day thinking about when he was a football player, playing games over in his mind."

He rolled away from her then, got as close to the edge of the bed as he could. "He's just like you," he said. "He's stuck back there too."

She had seen her daddy several times in between that Saturday night—when Chuckie walked into the kitchen murmuring "Mrs. Williams? Mrs. Williams?"—and the funeral, which was held at the Methodist church the following Wednesday morning. He had come to her grandmother's house Sunday evening, had gone into her grandmother's room and sat by the bed, holding her hand and sobbing. Dee Ann remained in the living room, and she heard their voices, heard her daddy saying, "Remember how she had those big rings under her eyes after Dee Ann was born? How we all said she looked like a pretty little racoon?" Her grandmother, whose chest pains had finally stopped, said, "Oh, Allen, I raised her from the cradle, and I know her well. She never would've stopped loving you." Then her daddy started crying again, and her grandmother joined in.

When he came out and walked down the hall to the living room, he had stopped crying, but his eyes were red-rimmed and his face looked puffy. He sat down in the armchair, which was still standing right where the sheriff had left it that afternoon. For a long time he said nothing. Then he rested his elbows on his knees, propped his chin on his fists, and said, "Were you the one that found her?"

"Chuckie did."

"Did you go in there?"

She nodded.

"He's an asshole for letting you do that."

She didn't bother to tell him how she'd torn herself out of Chuckie's grasp and bolted into the kitchen, or what had happened when she got in there. She was already starting to think what she would later know for certain: in the kitchen she had died. When she saw the pool of blood on the linoleum, saw the streaks that shot like flames up the wall, a thousand-volt jolt hit her heart. She lost her breath, and the room went dark, and when it relit itself she was somebody else.

Her momma's body lay in a lump on the floor, over by the door that led to the back porch. The shotgun that had killed her, her daddy's Remington Wingmaster, stood propped against the kitchen counter. Back in what had once been called the game room, the sheriff would find that somebody had pulled down all the guns—six rifles, the other shotgun, both of her daddy's .38s—and thrown them on the floor. He'd broken the lock on the metal cabinet that stood nearby, and he'd removed the box of shells and loaded the Remington.

It was hard to say what he'd been after, this man who for her was still a dark, faceless form. Her momma's purse had been ransacked, her wallet was missing, but there couldn't have been much money in it. She had some jewelry in the bedroom, but he hadn't messed with that. The most valuable things in the house were probably the guns themselves, but he hadn't taken them.

He'd come in through the back door—the lock was broken—and he'd left through the back door. Why Butch hadn't taken his leg off was anybody's guess. When the sheriff and his deputies showed up, it was all Chuckie could do to keep the dog from attacking.

"She wouldn't of wanted you to see her like that," her daddy said. "Nor me either." He spread his hands and looked at them, turning them over and scrutinizing his palms, as if he intended to read his own fortune. "I reckon I was lucky," he said, letting his gaze meet hers. "Anything you want to tell me about it?"

She shook her head no. The thought of telling him how she felt seemed somehow unreal. It had been years since she'd told him how she felt about anything that mattered.

"Life's too damn short," he said. "Our family's become one of those statistics you read about in the papers. You read those stories and you think it won't ever be you. Truth is, there's no way to insure against it."

At the time, the thing that struck her as odd was his use of the word *family*. They hadn't been a family for a long time, not as far as she was concerned.

She forgot about what he'd said until a few days later. What she remembered about that visit with him on Sunday night was that for the second time in twenty-four hours, he pulled her close and hugged her and gave her twenty dollars.

She saw him again Monday at the funeral home, and the day after that, and then the next day, at the funeral, she sat between him and her grandmother, and he held her hand while the preacher prayed. She had wondered if he would bring his girlfriend, but even he must have realized that would be inappropriate.

He apparently did not think it inappropriate, though,

or unwise either, to present himself at the offices of an insurance company in Jackson on Friday morning, bringing with him her mother's death certificate and a copy of the coroner's report.

When she thinks of the morning—a Saturday—on which Wheeler came to see her for the second time, she always imagines her own daughter sitting there on the couch at her grandmother's place instead of her. She sees Cynthia looking at the silver badge on Wheeler's shirt pocket, sees her glancing at the small notebook that lies open in his lap, at the pen gripped so tightly between his fingers that his knuckles have turned white.

"Now the other night," she hears Wheeler say, "your boyfriend picked you up at what time?"

"Right around eight o'clock." Her voice is weak, close to breaking. She just talked to her boyfriend an hour ago, and he was scared. His parents were pissed—pissed at Wheeler, pissed at him, but above all pissed at her. If she hadn't been dating their son, none of them would have been subjected to the awful experience they've just gone through this morning. They're devout Baptists, they don't drink or smoke, they've never seen the inside of a night-club, their names have never before been associated with unseemly acts. Now the sheriff has entered their home and questioned their son as if he were a common criminal. It will cost the sheriff their votes come November. She's already lost their votes. She lost them when her daddy left her momma and started running around with a young girl.

"The reason I'm kind of stuck on this eight o'clock

business," Wheeler says, "is you say that along about that time's when your daddy was there to see you."

"Yes, sir."

"Now your boyfriend claims he didn't see your daddy leaving the store. Says he didn't even notice the MG on the street."

"Daddy'd been gone a few minutes already. Plus, I think he parked around back."

"Parked around back," the sheriff says.

"Yes, sir."

"In that lot over by the bayou."

Even more weakly: "Yes, sir."

"Where the delivery trucks come in—ain't that where they usually park?"

"I believe so. Yes, sir."

Wheeler's pen pauses. He lays it on his knee. He turns his hands over, studying them as her daddy did his a few days before. He's looking at his hands when he asks the next question. "Any idea why your daddy'd park his car behind the grocery store—where there generally don't nothing but delivery trucks park—when Main Street was almost deserted and there was a whole row of empty spaces right in front of the store?"

The sheriff knows the answer as well as she does. When you're with a woman you're not married to, you don't park your car on Main Street on a Saturday night. Particularly if it's a little MG with no top on it, and your daughter's just a few feet away, with nothing but a pane of glass between her and a girl who's not much older than she is. That's how she explains it to herself anyway. At least for today.

"I think maybe he had his girlfriend with him."

"Well, I don't aim to hurt your feelings, honey," Wheeler says, looking at her now, "but there's not too many people that don't know about his girlfriend."

"Yes, sir."

"You reckon he might have parked out back for any other reason?"

She can't answer that question, so she doesn't even try.

"There's not any chance, is there," he says, "that your boyfriend could've been confused about when he picked you up?"

"No, sir."

"You're sure about that?"

She knows that Wheeler has asked Chuckie where he was between 7:15, when several people saw her mother eating a burger at the Sonic Drive-in, and 8:30, when the two of them found her body. Chuckie has told Wheeler he was at home watching TV between 7:15 and a few minutes till 8:00, when he got in the car and went to pick up Dee Ann. His parents were in Greenville eating supper at that time, so they can't confirm his story.

"Yes, sir," she says, "I'm sure about it."

"And you're certain your daddy was there just a few minutes before eight?"

"Yes, sir."

"Because your daddy," the sheriff says, "remembers things just a little bit different. The way your daddy remembers it, he came by the grocery store about 7:30 and hung around there talking with you for half an hour. Course, Mr. Lindsey was in the back, so he can't say yea or nay, and the stock boy don't seem to have the sense God give a betsy bug. Your daddy was over at the VFW drinking beer at eight o'clock—stayed there till almost ten, according to any number of people, and his girl-friend wasn't with him. Fact is, his girlfriend left the country last Thursday morning. Took a flight from New Orleans to Mexico City, and from there it looks like she went on to Argentina."

Dee Ann, imagining this scene in which her daughter reprises the role she once played, sees Cynthia's face go slack as the full force of the information strikes her. She's still sitting there like that—hands useless in her lap, face drained of blood—when Jim Wheeler tells her that six months ago, her daddy took out a life insurance policy on her momma that includes double indemnity in the event of accidental death.

"I hate to be the one telling you this, honey," he says, "because you're a girl who's had enough bad news to last the rest of her life. But your daddy stands to collect half a million dollars because of your momma's death, and there's a number of folks—and I reckon I might as well admit I happen to be among them—who are starting to think that ought not to occur."

Chuckie gets off work at Delta Electric at six o'clock. A year or so ago she became aware that he'd started coming home late. The first time it happened, he told her he'd gone out with his friend Tim to have a beer. She saw Tim the next day buying a case of motor oil at Wal-Mart, and she almost referred to his and Chuckie's night out just to see if he looked surprised. But if he'd looked surprised, it would have worried her, and if he hadn't, it would have worried her even more: she would have seen it as a sign that Chuckie had talked to him beforehand. So in the end she nodded at Tim and kept her mouth shut.

It began happening more and more often. Chuckie ran over to Greenville to buy some parts for his truck, he ran down to Yazoo City for a meeting with his regional supervisor. He ran up into the north part of the county because a fellow who lived there had placed an interesting ad in *National Rifleman*—he was selling a shotgun with fancy scrollwork on the stock.

On the evenings when Chuckie isn't home, she avoids latching onto Cynthia. She wants her daughter to have her own life, to be independent, even if independence, in a sixteen-year-old girl, manifests itself as distance from her mother. Cynthia is on the phone a lot, talking to girlfriends, to boyfriends too. Through the bedroom door Dee Ann hears her laughter.

On the evenings when Chuckie isn't home, she sits on the couch alone, watching TV, reading, or listening to music. If it's a Friday or Saturday night and Cynthia is out with her friends, Dee Ann goes out herself. She doesn't go to movies, where her presence might make Cynthia feel crowded if she happened to be in the theater too, and she doesn't go out and eat at any of the handful of restaurants in town. Instead she takes long walks. Sometimes they last until ten or eleven o'clock.

Every now and then, when she's on one of these walks, passing one house after another where families sit parked before the TV set, she allows herself to wish she had a dog to keep her company. What she won't allow herself to do—has never allowed herself to do as an adult—is actually own one.

The arrest of her father is preserved in a newspaper photo.

He has just gotten out of Sheriff Wheeler's car. The car stands parked in the alleyway between the courthouse and the fire station. Sheriff Wheeler is in the picture too, standing just to the left of her father, and so is one of his deputies. The deputy has his hand on her father's right forearm, and he is staring straight into the camera, as is Sheriff Wheeler. Her daddy is the only one who appears not to notice that his picture is being taken. He is looking off to the left, in the direction of Loring Street, which you can't see in the photo, though she knows it's there.

When she takes the photo out and examines it, something she does with increasing frequency these days, she wonders why her daddy is not looking at the camera. A reasonable conclusion, she knows, would be that since he's about to be arraigned on murder charges, he doesn't want his face in the paper. But she wonders if there isn't more to it. He doesn't look particularly worried. He's not exactly smiling, but there aren't a lot of lines around his mouth, like there would be if he felt especially tense. Were he not wearing handcuffs, were he not flanked on either side by officers of the law, you would probably have to say he looks relaxed.

Then there's the question of what he's looking at. Lou Pierce's office is on Loring Street, and Loring Street is what's off the page, out of the picture. Even if the photographer had wanted to capture it in this photo, he couldn't have, not as long as he was intent on capturing the images of these three men. By choosing to photograph them, he chose not to photograph something else, and

sometimes what's outside the frame may be more important than what's actually in it.

After all, Loring Street is south of the alley. And so is
Argentina.

"You think he'd do that?" Chuckie said. "You think
he'd actually kill your momma?"

They were sitting in his pickup when he asked her that
question. The pickup was parked on a turnrow in somebody's cotton patch on a Saturday afternoon in August.
By then her daddy had been in jail for the better part of
two weeks. The judge had denied him bail, apparently
believing that he aimed to leave the country. The judge
couldn't have known that her daddy had no intention of
leaving the country without the insurance money, which
had been placed in an escrow account and wouldn't be
released until he'd been cleared of the murder charges.

The cotton patch they were parked in was way up
close to Cleveland. Chuckie's parents had forbidden him
to go out with Dee Ann again, so she'd hiked out to the
highway, and he'd picked her up on the side of the road.
In later years she'll often wonder whether or not she and
Chuckie would have stayed together and gotten married
if his parents hadn't placed her off-limits.

"I don't know," she said. "He sure did lie about coming
to see me. And then there's Butch. If somebody broke in,
he'd tear them to pieces. But he wouldn't hurt Daddy."

"I don't believe it," Chuckie said. A can of Bud stood
clamped between his thighs. He lifted it and took a swig.
"Your daddy may have acted a little wacky, running off
like he did and taking up with that girl, but to shoot your

momma and then come in the grocery store and grin at you? You really think *anybody* could do a thing like that?"

What Dee Ann was beginning to think was that almost everybody could do a thing like that. She didn't know why this was so, but she believed it had something to do with being an adult and having ties. Having ties meant you were bound to certain things—certain people, certain places, certain ways of living. Breaking a tie was a violent act—even if all you did was walk out door number one and enter door number two—and one act of violence could lead to another. You didn't have to spill blood to take a life. But after taking a life, you still might spill blood, if spilling blood would get you something else you wanted.

"I don't know what he might have done," she said.

"Every time I was ever around him," Chuckie said, "he was in a nice mood. I remember going in the flower shop with momma when I was just a kid. Your daddy was always polite and friendly. Used to give me lollipops."

"Yeah, well, he never gave me any lollipops. And besides, your momma used to be real pretty."

"What's that supposed to mean?"

"It's not supposed to mean anything. I'm just stating a fact."

"You saying she's not pretty now?"

His innocence startled her. If she handled him right, Dee Ann realized, she could make him do almost anything she wanted. For an instant she was tempted to put her hand inside his shirt, stroke his chest a couple of times, and tell him to climb out of the truck and stand on his head. She wouldn't always have such leverage, but she had it now, and a voice in her head urged her to exploit it.

"I'm not saying she's not pretty anymore," Dee Ann said. "I'm just saying that of course Daddy was nice to her. He was always nice to nice-looking women."

"Your momma was a nice-looking lady too."

"Yeah, but my momma was his wife."

Chuckie turned away and gazed out at the cotton patch for several seconds. When he looked back at her, he said, "You know what, Dee Ann? You're not making much sense." He took another sip of beer, then pitched the can out the window. "But with all you've been through," he said, starting the engine, "I don't wonder at it."

He laid his hand on her knee. It stayed there until twenty minutes later, when he let her out on the highway, right where he'd picked her up.

Sometimes in her mind she has trouble separating all the men. It's as if they're revolving around her, her daddy and Chuckie and Jim Wheeler and Lou Pierce and Barry Lancaster, as if she's sitting motionless in a hard chair, in a small room, and they're orbiting her so fast that their faces blur into a single image that seems suspended just inches away. She smells them too: smells aftershave and cologne, male sweat and whiskey.

Lou Pierce was a man she'd been seeing around town for as long as she could remember. He always wore a striped long-sleeved shirt and a wide tie that was usually loud-colored. You would see him crossing Loring Street, a coffee cup in one hand, his briefcase in the other. His office was directly across the street from the courthouse, where he spent much of his life—either visiting his clients in the jail, which was on the top floor, or defending those same clients downstairs in the courtroom itself.

Many years after he represented her father, Lou Pierce would find himself up on the top floor again, on the other side of the bars this time, accused of exposing himself to a twelve-year-old girl. After the story made the paper, several other women, most in their twenties or early thirties, would contact the local police and allege that he had also shown himself to them.

He showed himself to Dee Ann too, though not the same part of himself he showed to the twelve-year-old girl. He came to see her at her grandmother's on a weekday evening sometime after the beginning of the fall semester—she knows school was in session because she remembers that the morning after Lou Pierce visited her, she had to sit beside his son Raymond in senior English.

Lou sat in the same armchair that Jim Wheeler had pulled up near the coffee table. He didn't have his briefcase with him, but he was wearing another of those wide ties. This one, if she remembers correctly, had a pink background, with white fleurs-de-lis.

"How you making it, honey?" he says. "You been holding up all right?"

She shrugs. "Yes, sir. I guess so."

"Your daddy's awful worried about you." He picks up the cup of coffee her grandmother brought him before leaving them alone. "I don't know if you knew that or not," he says, taking a sip of the coffee. He sets the cup back down. "He mentioned you haven't been to see him."

He's gazing directly at her, and his big droopy eyelids give him a lost-doggy look.

"No, sir," she says, "I haven't gotten by there."

"You know what that makes folks think, don't you?"

She drops her head. "No, sir."

"Makes 'em think you believe your daddy did it."

That's the last thing he says for two or three minutes. He sits there sipping his coffee, looking around the room, almost as if he were a real estate agent sizing up the house. Just as she decides he's said all he intends to, his voice comes back at her.

"Daddies fail," he tells her. "Lordy, how we fail. You could ask Raymond. I doubt he'd tell the truth, though, because sons tend to be protective of their daddies, just like a good daughter protects her momma. But the truth, if you wanted to dig into it, is that I've failed that boy nearly every day he's been alive. You notice he's in the band? Hell, he can't kick a football or hit a baseball, and that's nobody's fault but mine. I remember when he was this tall—" he holds his hand, palm down, three feet from the floor "—he came to me dragging this little plastic bat and said, 'Daddy, teach me to hit a baseball.' And you know what I told him? I told him, 'Son, I'm defending a man that's facing life in prison, and I got to go before the judge tomorrow morning and plead his case. You can take that bat and you can hitch a kite to it and see if the contraption won't fly.'"

He reaches across the table then and lays his hand on her knee. She tries to remember who else has done that recently, but for the moment she can't recall.

When he speaks again, he keeps his voice low, as if he's afraid he'll be overheard. "Dee Ann, what I'm telling you," he says, "is I know there are a lot of things about your daddy that make you feel conflicted. There's a lot of things he's done that he shouldn't have, and there's things he should have done that he didn't. There's a bunch of *shoulds* and *shouldn'ts* bumping around in your head, so it's no surprise to me that you'd get confused on this question of time."

She's heard people say that if they're ever guilty of a crime, they want Lou Pierce to defend them. Now she knows why.

But she's not guilty of a crime, and she says so: "I'm not confused about time. He came when I said he did."

As if she's a sworn witness, Lou Pierce begins, gently, regretfully, to ask her a series of questions. Does she really think her daddy is stupid enough to take out a life insurance policy on her mother and then kill her? If he aimed to leave the country with his girlfriend, would he send the girl first and then kill Dee Ann's momma and try to claim the money? Does she know that her daddy intended to put the money in a savings account for her?

Does she know that her daddy and his girlfriend had already broken up, that the girl left the country chasing some young South American who, her daddy has admitted, probably sold her drugs?

When he sees that she isn't going to answer any of the questions, Lou Pierce looks down at the floor. It's as if he already knows that one day he'll find himself in a predicament similar to her father's: sitting in a small dark cell, accused of something shameful. "Honey," he says softly, "did you ever ask yourself why your daddy left you and your momma?"

That's one question she's willing and able to answer. "He did it because he didn't love us."

When he looks at her again, his eyes are wet—and she

hasn't yet learned that wet eyes tell the most effective lies. "He loved y'all," Lou Pierce says. "But your momma, who was a wonderful lady—angel, she wouldn't give your daddy a physical life. I guarantee you he wishes to God he hadn't needed one, but a man's not made that way . . . and even though it embarrasses me, I guess I ought to add that I'm speaking from personal experience."

Personal experience.

At the age of thirty-eight, Dee Ann has acquired a wealth of experience, but the phrase *personal experience* is one she almost never uses. She's noticed that men are a lot quicker to employ it than women are. Maybe it's because men think their experiences are somehow more personal than everybody else's. Or maybe it's because they take everything personally.

"My own personal experience," Chuckie told Cynthia the other day at the dinner table, after she'd finished ninth in the voting for one of eight positions on the cheerleading squad, "has been that getting elected cheerleader's nothing more than a popularity contest, and I wouldn't let not getting elected worry me for two seconds."

Dee Ann couldn't help it. "When in the world," she said, "did you have a *personal* experience with a cheerleader election?"

He laid his fork down. They stared at one another across a bowl of spaghetti. Cynthia, who can detect a developing storm front as well as any meteorologist, wiped her mouth on her napkin, stood up and said, "Excuse me."

Chuckie kept his mouth shut until she'd left the room. "I *voted* in cheerleader elections."

"What was personal about that experience?"

"It was my own personal vote."

"Did you have any emotional investment in that vote?"

"You ran once. I voted for you. I was emotional about you then."

She didn't even question him about his use of the word *then*—she knew perfectly well why he used it. "And when I didn't win," she said, "you took it personally?"

"I felt bad for you."

"But not nearly as bad as you felt for yourself?"

"Why in the hell would I feel bad for myself?"

"Having a girlfriend who couldn't win a popularity contest—wasn't that hard on you? Didn't you take it personally?"

He didn't answer. He just sat there looking at her over the bowl of spaghetti, his eyes hard as sandstone and every bit as dry.

Cynthia walks home from school, and several times in the last couple of years, Dee Ann, driving through town on her way back from a shopping trip or a visit to the library, has come across her daughter. Cynthia hunches over as she walks, her canvas backpack slung over her right shoulder, her eyes studying the sidewalk as if she's trying to figure out the pavement's composition. She may be thinking about her boyfriend or some idle piece of gossip she heard that day at school, or she may be trying to remember if the fourth president was James Madison or James Monroe, but her posture and the concentrated way she gazes down suggest that she's a girl who believes she has a problem.

Whether or not this is so Dee Ann doesn't know, because if her daughter is worried about something she's never mentioned it. What Dee Ann does know is that whenever she's out driving and she sees Cynthia walking home, she always stops the car, rolls her window down and says, "Want a ride?" Cynthia always looks up and smiles, not the least bit startled, and she always says yes. She's never once said no, like Dee Ann did to three different people that day twenty years ago, when, instead of walking to her grandmother's after school, she walked all the way from the highway to the Loring County courthouse and climbed the front steps and stood staring at the heavy oak door for several seconds before she pushed it open.

Her daddy has gained weight. His cheeks have grown round, the backs of his hands are plump. He's not getting any exercise to speak of. On Tuesday and Wednesday nights, he tells her, the prisoners who want to keep in shape are let out of their cells, one at a time, and allowed to jog up and down three flights of stairs for ten minutes each. He says an officer sits in a straight-backed chair down in the courthouse lobby with a rifle across his lap to make sure that the prisoners don't jog any farther.

Her daddy is sitting on the edge of his cot. He's wearing blue denim pants and a shirt to match, and a patch on the pocket of the shirt says *Loring County Jail.* The shoes he has on aren't really shoes. They look like bedroom slippers.

Downstairs, when she checked in with the jailer, Jim

Wheeler heard her voice and came out of his office. While she waited for the jailer to get the right key, the sheriff asked her how she was doing.

"All right, I guess."

"You may think I'm lying, honey," he said, "but the day'll come when you'll look back on this time in your life and it won't seem like nothing but a real bad dream."

Sitting in a hard plastic chair, looking at her father, she already feels like she's in a bad dream. He's smiling at her, waiting for her to say something, but her tongue feels like it's stuck to the roof of her mouth.

The jail is air-conditioned, but it's hot in the cell, and the place smells bad. The toilet over in the corner has no lid on it. She wonders how in the name of God a person can eat in a place like this. And what kind of person could actually eat enough to gain weight?

As if he knows what she's thinking, her father says, "You're probably wondering how I can stand it."

She doesn't answer.

"I can stand it," he says, "because I know I deserved to be locked up."

He sits there a moment longer, then gets up off the cot and shuffles over to the window, which has three bars across it. He stands there looking out. "All my life," he finally says, "I've been going in and out of all those buildings down there and I never once asked myself what they looked like from above. Now I know. There's garbage on those roofs and bird shit. One day I saw a man sitting up there, drinking from a paper bag. Right on top of Delta Jewelers."

He turns around then and walks over and lays his hand on her shoulder.

"When I was down there," he says, "scurrying around like a chicken with its head cut off, I never gave myself enough time to think. That's one thing I've had plenty of in here. And I can tell you, I've seen some things I was too blind to see then."

He keeps his hand on her shoulder the whole time he's talking. "In the last few weeks," he says, "I've asked myself how you must have felt when I told you I was too busy to play with you, how you probably felt every time you had to go to the picture show by yourself and you saw all those other little girls waiting in line with their daddies and holding their hands." He says he's seen all the ways in which he failed them both, her and her mother, and he knows they both saw them a long time ago. He just wishes to God *he* had.

He takes his hand off her shoulder, goes back over to the cot and sits down. She watches, captivated, as his eyes begin to glisten. She realizes that she's in the presence of a man capable of anything, and for the first time she knows the answer to a question that has always baffled her: why would her momma put up with so much for so long?

The answer is that her daddy is a natural performer, and her momma was his natural audience. Her momma lived for these routines, she watched till watching killed her.

With watery eyes, Dee Ann's daddy looks at her, here in a stinking room in the Loring County courthouse. "Sweetheart," he whispers, "you don't think I killed her, do you?"

When she speaks, her voice will be steady, it won't crack and break. She will display no more emotion than if she were responding to a question posed by her history teacher.

"No, sir," she tells her daddy. "I don't think you killed her. I *know* you did."

In that instant the weight of his life begins to crush her.

Ten-thirty on a Saturday night in 1997. She's standing alone in an alleyway outside the courthouse. It's the same alley where her father and Jim Wheeler and the deputy had their picture taken all those years ago. Loring is the same town it was then, except now there are gangs, and gunfire is something you hear all week long, not just on Saturday night. Now people kill folks they don't know.

Chuckie is supposedly at a deer camp with some men she's never met. He told her he knows them from a sporting goods store in Greenville. They all started talking about deer hunting, and one of the men told Chuckie he owned a cabin over behind the levee and suggested Chuckie go hunting with them this year.

Cynthia is out with her friends—she may be at a movie or she may be in somebody's backseat. Wherever she is, Dee Ann prays she's having fun. She prays that Cynthia's completely caught up in whatever she's doing and that she won't come along and find her momma here, standing alone in the alley beside the Loring County courthouse, gazing up through the darkness as though she hopes to read the stars.

The room reminds her of a Sunday-school classroom. It's on the second floor of the courthouse, overlooking the alley. There's a long wooden table in the middle of the room, and she's sitting at one end of it in a straight-backed chair. Along both sides, in similar chairs, sit fifteen men and women who make up the Loring County grand jury. She knows several faces, three or four names. It looks as if every one of them is drinking coffee. They've all got styrofoam cups.

Down at the far end of the table, with a big manila folder open in front of him, sits Barry Lancaster, the district attorney, a man whose name she's going to be seeing in newspaper articles a lot in the next twenty years. He's just turned thirty, and though it's still warm out, he's wearing a black suit, with a sparkling white shirt and a glossy black tie.

Barry Lancaster has the reputation of being tough on crime, and he's going to ride that reputation all the way to the state attorney general's office and then to a federal judgeship. When he came to see her a few days ago, it was his reputation that concerned him. After using a lot of phrases like "true bill" and "no bill" without bothering to explain precisely what they meant, he said, "My reputation's at stake here, Dee Ann. There's a whole lot riding on you."

She knows how much is riding on her, and it's a lot more than his reputation. She feels the great mass bearing down on her shoulders. Her neck is stiff and her legs are heavy. She didn't sleep last night. She never really sleeps anymore.

"Now Dee Ann," Barry Lancaster says, "we all know you've gone through a lot recently, but I need to ask you some questions today so that these ladies and gentlemen can hear your answers. Will that be okay?"

She wants to say that it's not okay, that it will never again be okay for anyone to ask her anything, but she just nods.

He asks her how old she is.

"Eighteen."

What grade she's in.

"I'm a senior."

Whether or not she has a boyfriend named Chuckie Nelms.

"Yes, sir."

Whether or not, on Saturday evening, August 2, she saw her boyfriend.

"Yes, sir."

Barry Lancaster looks up from the stack of papers and smiles at her. "If I was your boyfriend," he says, "I'd want to see you *every* night."

A few of the men on the grand jury grin, but the women keep straight faces. One of them, a small red-headed woman with lots of freckles, whose name she doesn't know and never will know, is going to wait on her in a convenience store over in Indianola many years later. After giving her change, the woman will touch Dee Ann's hand and say, "I hope the rest of your life's been easier, honey. It must have been awful, what you went through."

Barry Lancaster takes her through that Saturday evening, from the time Chuckie picked her up until the moment when she walked into the kitchen. Then he asks her, in a solemn voice, what she found there.

She keeps her eyes trained on his tie pin, a small amethyst, as she describes the scene in as much detail as she can muster. In a roundabout way, word will reach her that many of the people on the grand jury were shocked, and even appalled, at her lack of emotion. Chuckie will try to downplay their reaction, telling her that they're probably just saying that because of what happened later on. "It's probably not you they're reacting to," he'll say. "It's probably just them having hindsight."

Hindsight is something she lacks, as she sits here in a hard chair, in a small room, her hands lying before her on a badly scarred table. She can't make a bit of sense out of what's already happened. She knows what her daddy was and she knows what he wasn't, knows what he did and didn't do. What she doesn't know is the whys and the wherefores.

On the other hand, she can see into the future, she knows what's going to happen, and she also knows why. She knows, for instance, what question is coming, and she knows how she's going to answer it and why. She knows that shortly after she's given that answer, Barry Lancaster will excuse her, and she knows, because Lou Pierce has told her, that after she's been excused, Barry Lancaster will address the members of the grand jury.

He will tell them what they have and haven't heard. "Now she's a young girl," he'll say, "and she's been through a lot, and in the end this case has to rest on what she can tell us. And the truth, ladies and gentlemen, much as I might want it to be otherwise, is that the kid's gone shaky on us. She told the sheriff one version of what happened at the grocery store that Saturday night when her daddy came to see her, and she's sat here today and told y'all a different version. She's gotten all confused on this question of time. You can't blame her for that, she's young and her mind's troubled, but in all honesty a good defense attorney's apt to rip my case apart. Because when you lose this witness's testimony, all you've got left is that dog, and that dog, ladies and gentlemen, can't testify."

That dog can't testify.

Even as she sits here, waiting for Barry Lancaster to bring up that night in the grocery store—that night which, for her, will always be the present—she knows the statement about the dog will be used to sentence Jim Wheeler to November defeat. The voters of this county will drape that sentence around the sheriff's neck. If Jim Wheeler had done his job and found some real evidence, they will say, that man would be on his way to Parchman.

They will tell one another, the voters of this county, how someone saw her daddy at the Jackson airport, as he boarded a plane that would take him to Dallas, where he would board yet another plane for a destination farther south. They will say that her daddy was actually carrying a briefcase filled with money, with lots of crisp green hundreds, one of which he extracted to pay for a beer.

They will say that her daddy must have paid her to lie, that she didn't give a damn about her mother. They will wonder if Chuckie has a brain in his head, to go and marry somebody like her, and they will ask themselves how she can ever bear the shame of what she's done. They will not believe, not even for a moment, that she's performed some careful calculations in her mind. All that shame, she's decided, will still weigh a lot less than her daddy's life. It will be a while before she and Chuckie and a girl who isn't born yet learn how much her faulty math has cost.

Barry Lancaster makes a show of rifling through his papers. He pulls a sheet out and studies it, lets his face wrinkle up as if he's seeing something on the page that he never saw before. Then he lays the sheet back down. He closes the manila folder, pushes his chair away from the table a few inches and leans forward. She's glad he's too far away to lay his hand on her knee.

"Now," he says, "let's go backwards in time."

The Atlas Bone

I **WAS STILL** married at the time. We were living in a two-bedroom house in McCabe, Texas, and I was stationed at the McCabe Naval Air Station. I flew the F-18.

I say I was stationed there, and I say we lived there, but insofar as this story goes, both statements may be a little misleading. We'd only been there a short time when Operation Desert Storm got under way. I'd hardly had a chance to move in before I was gone.

But the letters I received from Trudi during those five months I was away made it clear she had a problem with the house. Or to be more precise, she had a problem with the location of the house.

Trudi's German. She's tall and blonde and, in general, very direct. When we got transferred to McCabe, she let everybody know right away that she thought west Texas was the ugliest spot on the face of the Earth.

"Everything is flat and dry here," she said. "No wonder they chose this place for an air base. They probably believed a few plane crashes would add color to the landscape."

When she first started to complain in her letters, I assumed McCabe itself was the problem. It is an ugly place; it's small and there's not much going on there, and the closest real town is Abilene—and what can you say about it? But gradually it became clear that her environmental problem was even more immediate.

I don't like to complain, she finally wrote. *I know you are risking your life for Texaco. But we have bought a house next door to a terrible person. If Hermann Göring had lived in McCabe, our neighbor is the man he would have been.*

I'd seen the guy and his wife when we moved in. Like Trudi, the woman was a foreigner, from Venezuela, it turned out. She had olive-colored skin, long brown hair. You could tell she liked to keep in shape. I'd seen her leave the house first thing in the morning, dressed in a tight black gym suit.

The woman's husband, the object of Trudi's displeasure, was configured very differently from his wife. He was in his late thirties, sandy-haired, with a reddish face that looked as if, in its youth, it had been carpet bombed by acne. He was about six feet tall, and I would have put his weight at right around three hundred. It looked like walking across the yard left him winded. When he climbed into his car, a little white Civic, you wondered if the shocks would survive. The real estate agent who sold us the house had said he was a doctor.

The first week we lived there, Trudi got a bad cold. Not wanting to wait for an appointment at the base, she chose a GP at random. She ended up at our neighbor's office. Doug Hench, his name was. While sitting in his waiting room along with one other patient, a guy in his twenties who wore a pair of Wranglers, along with a plaid shirt and a cowboy hat, she had heard Doug on the phone.

"You're damn right it's venereal," he said. His voice really carried. "It's about as venereal as anything I ever saw."

A brief silence followed.

"Hell yes," he said. "I've got a dental mirror stuck in there right now and I can see plenty. Believe me, this lady's got a problem. Can you work her in this afternoon?"

Trudi was on her feet. As she left the office, the guy with the cowboy hat said, "I'm gonna stick around and see who the patient is so I can stay *away* from her."

In the middle of the night, Trudi wrote in her letter, *he wakes me up chopping wood. Our house starts to shake. If I holler at him to be quiet, he quits, but the next night he does it again. Yesterday, I peeped through the cracks in the fence, and I could see that the wood is stacked up right next to it. A distance of three feet separates our bed from this man's wood pile.*

When she was looking through the cracks, Trudi wrote, he came out of his house. His backyard, like ours, had a wooden fence all the way around it, so it couldn't be seen from the street. He was naked. Trudi said she had never seen so much body hair on a living creature, except for the time her father took her to the Dortmund Zoo.

I miss you, Trudi continued. *Please don't get killed. Don't do anything to make your father proud. If they shoot you*

*down, surrender. Say everything they want—don't even wait
for them to tell you what it is. Just ask them: What can I say
or do to make you happy?*

And what, I wanted to ask her, can I say or do to make
you happy? I'd moved her in next to a wood-chopping
lunatic, who might also be an exhibitionist, and then I'd
left. And as always when things weren't going well, Trudi
cast an eye in the direction of my father, the retired admiral, who, upon my graduation from Annapolis, had stood
so stiff and so proud for so long that his back went into a
spasm and a medic had to shoot him full of Flexeril.

I didn't get killed—I didn't even come close. The only
time I saw Baghdad was on CNN. The carrier I was stationed on floated around the Mediterranean for four and
a half months. My squadron was always about to be engaged, but it never was. Then the war ended, and we
headed for McCabe.

If Dad had been a different sort of retired admiral, he
might have picked up the phone and given somebody an
earful. But that would have constituted an attempt to
subvert command. "You'll get another chance," he said
on the phone. Somehow he sounded as if he didn't quite
believe it. He sounded as if he feared all the tyrants might
behave.

The first few days back were, as always, strained. Trudi
had been sleeping on the left side of the bed, because that
was the one farthest from Doug Hench's property and she
wanted to stay as far away from Doug as she could. But
the left side had traditionally been my side. I told her I
didn't mind sleeping close to the wall, but Trudi came

from the Old World and was not someone who would willfully ignore tradition.

So she went back to the right side. Even though it was April by then, and Doug had quit chopping wood, she couldn't sleep. She tossed and turned, rolled and kicked, and kept me awake until two or three o'clock. What we needed, both of us, was some relaxation.

Our property had come with a hot tub, which until now we hadn't used. Trudi had been intending to get in it, but the notion that Doug might peek through the fence at her, just as she'd peeked through at him, had kept her away from it. The first Friday I was back, I went out into the backyard and cleaned the tub out good and then filled it and turned on the heater. Later I drove to the store and bought some ribs and a six-pack of beer. While Trudi took a nap, I basted the ribs and made a big salad, then I went out back and fired up my gas grill. Afterwards I checked the water in the hot tub. It was perfect.

I woke her up and told her we were going to have a cookout, and that improved her mood. She helped me carry the ribs out back. I put them on and cooked them nice and slow, and we sat in lawn chairs drinking beer and talking about the day we'd met. It had happened in Norfolk, Virginia, where I was stationed at the time. Trudi was there to visit her aunt, who was a friend of my mother's. We met at a cookout.

"Just like this," I said, laying my hand on her knee.

She started to sip her beer. Halfway to her mouth, the bottle stopped. "Not just like this," she said.

"Why not?"

I had the impression she was staring at something behind me. I turned and looked over my shoulder.

The head of Doug Hench, round as a pumpkin, seemed to sit atop the fence. He must have been standing on something. His woodpile, maybe.

"Home is the hunter, hail from the sea, come back from making the world safe for me." He raised a beer bottle, waved it at us. "Cheers," he said.

Later that night Trudi would ask me why I had done what I did next. I wouldn't be able to tell her, because I didn't know myself. I didn't know then, but I do know now, and the answer is this: I did it because for many months, I had been on an aircraft carrier, surrounded by men I had to believe I could depend on. Many of these men had names I didn't know. They might have held beliefs that would have been repulsive to me. There might have been thieves among them, a murderer or two maybe, perhaps even a purveyor of kiddie porn. But if any one of them had called to me in need, I would have responded.

I believe I did what I did that night because Doug Hench was a man, and I was a man, and I knew that Doug Hench was in need. I raised my beer bottle and nodded at Doug and said, "Cheers."

And then Doug said, "Mind if we join you?"

Couples. Neighbors. Four people getting together in the backyard to enjoy food, drink, friendship.

It was a vision of America Dad always promoted. "It's what makes this country great," he said. "Community. The ties that bind. Backyard barbecues." He promoted that vision even though the whole time I was growing up, we were on the move, traveling from Alabama to California, from Virginia to Florida and back. He promoted it even though, no matter where we were living, he invariably despised our neighbors, considering them soft and lazy, undisciplined and amoral. Most of them, he said, weren't fit to sweep decks. He would not have welcomed them into his own backyard any more than he would have welcomed Angela Davis or Huey P. Newton.

Doug Hench and his wife, Araceli, had joined us at our picnic table. Doug was already drunk when they walked through the gate, and over the next hour or so he got a lot drunker. He sat there in a pair of baggy gray shorts and a green T-shirt that was about to bust open.

He grabbed a rib—his sixth or seventh of the evening—and started gnawing it. Juice dripped down his chin and onto his T-shirt, which had long ago begun to look as if he'd dipped it in a vat of Crisco

Trudi wouldn't look at Araceli—she was probably too embarrassed for her. She couldn't bear to look at Doug, so she looked at me. And as she looked at me, I somehow knew that for her tonight had not been and would not be relaxing. If it had not relaxed her, it would not and could not relax me. She would again toss and roll. She would kick me in her sleep. I was beginning to miss the drone of engines, the thud that came from the deck when a plane touched down. It was better for the deck of a carrier to make that sound than for my shin to make it.

"In a way," Doug said, "being a doctor's a lot like being a pilot in combat."

"How's that?" I said.

"We both have to kill people."

"Kill them?" Trudi said.

"I never killed anybody," I said.

"You'll kill 'em," Doug said.

"Douglas," Araceli said.

"I pulled the plug on a fellow yesterday," he said. "Actually, it's not a plug. It's a hose. He was ninety-three. He'd had himself a dandy stroke about a month back. I gathered all his family members in the room, and I closed the door, and I said 'Okay, you all want his ticket punched. You want me to do the honors or would one of you like to?' They wanted me to."

The expression on Trudi's face was the one she would have worn if she had taken the lid off a pot and found a dead rat inside it. Her nose wrinkled up, her mouth twisted sideways. She said, "It's late."

"It's early," Doug said. He glanced at his watch. "Eight-thirty. Time to party down."

Araceli said, "I *am* sleepy."

"I am too," Trudi said.

She got up. Standing, she was an impressive sight. That night, as I recall, she had on tight shorts and a red silk blouse. The light from the back porch hit her hair just right. It sparkled. I wanted nothing so much as to be in bed with her right then.

"What about you?" she said, gazing down on me. "Aren't you sleepy? You must be."

Before I could say whether I was or wasn't sleepy, Doug Hench slapped my knee. "Hey, von Richthofen," he said, "is that a hot tub I see over there?"

At this point the women go off to bed, disappearing from the evening and from the story—just as a year later, while my squadron was on a six-month tour of duty in the Pacific, Trudi disappeared from my life. She returned to Germany, where she lives now with a Polish rock musician who, I hear, makes his living off a bunch of slot machines he owns in western Poland. Once every two weeks, so I'm told, he drives across the border for his zlotys.

Araceli disappeared from Doug's life too. She drove to Abilene three times a week for a couple of years, earned an accounting degree, filed for divorce, and set herself up as a CPA.

What's left, as far as the evening and the story go, are two naked guys in a hot tub, in the middle of west Texas, on a spring night in 1991. I got in first. Then Doug did, and at that point about a third of the water sloshed over the rim of the tub and onto the deck.

What, you might ask, were we doing in that tub? Was it, as Trudi would allege some hours later, that having spent the last several months floating in a large body of water with hundreds of men, I was attempting to duplicate the experience by lounging in the hot tub with Doug?

It was not. The truth was that my muscles were sore, and my legs hurt from the constant battering they had received the past few nights. I wanted to be in that tub, because I wanted to be in that tub. I would have preferred to be there with Trudi, or failing that, with Araceli. Of all the possibilities, the one I found least appealing was to be there with Doug. But Doug it was.

"You like what you do?" Doug said.

"I love it."

"What's so great about flying a tube of Crest?"

Locking my hands behind my head, I said a few words about service to one's country, about learning to do something that was not easy and do it well. I alluded to the joys of teamwork and praised the concepts of personal and national excellence.

And when I had finished, Doug Hench said, "Aw, horseshit."

"It is, isn't it?" I said.

It shocked me to hear myself say that. I thought instantly of my father. If he had heard me just now, his knees might have buckled.

"'Course it's horseshit," Doug said.

"So why do I do it?"

"Flying, you stand a fair chance of dying. Maybe you get off on knowing that."

I admitted that there was a certain kind of pleasure derived from the knowledge that no matter how far or how high you flew, you always had to come back down, which at any given time could pose a problem. I also confessed that once or twice the urge to tilt the nose up and climb until the engines flamed out had almost overcome me.

Still, I said, I didn't think I had a death wish. "I am what I always assumed I'd be. In the end that's about all the reason there is."

"Me," Doug said, "I do what I do for the worst reason in the world."

"Money?"

"Money?" Doug said. "Are you joking? I've got the poorest practice in west Texas. Ace, you're looking at a man who slobbers at the sight of the Medi-Care trough."

No, he said, his reason was much worse than money. When I asked him what it was, he began to tell a story.

He said his dad had gone to the University of Texas, and his grandfather had too, and both of them had been doctors. His dad, at one time, had been president of the Houston Medical Association—his practice had been the most successful in that city.

With a dad like that, Doug said, he should have been set. His father had been a personal friend of M. Philip Butts, the president of UT. Butts had dined at their home.

"When I went to Austin," Doug said, "Phil invited me over. I remember watching a football game with him in his den. *I'm in,* I thought, *I'm in.*"

He was in, all right, but it wasn't long before he was almost out. He liked to party. Without his father around to stop him, he indulged. He could show me a picture, he said, of himself as a three hundred-pound sophomore, clad in a pair of polka-dot bloomers, crawling across the quad, a beer pitcher balanced on his back. He flirted with probation for four long years, emerging with a pre-med degree and a flat 2.0. Medical schools were not impressed.

"But there was one down in Venezuela," he said, "that actively recruited American students." He spat out a bunch of words in Spanish. "The Cumana Institute of Medicine. Americans who had low GPA's could get in if they paid the entire tuition up front.

"I remember sitting down across the desk from Dad in his study. 'This is it,' he said. 'This is the last line of a play by Samuel Beckett. If you bomb down there—and you're bound to—don't come back.' "

"Well, you're a doctor now," I said. "You made your dad eat his words."

"No, I didn't—men like Dad eat filet mignon, they don't eat words. But I almost went to a Latin American prison trying."

Doug said all the new students at the institute started out with an anatomy class. It was taught by a man named Perez. Perez was in his fifties, stocky and dark-haired, and he wore a closely trimmed beard. He'd translated *Gray's Anatomy* into Spanish, put his own name on it, and made, according to Doug, a killing and a half. He arrived at work in a red Mercedes, and he had been seen around town with a bunch of different women, all of them beautiful, many of them foreign, most of them young.

The anatomy class met in a quonset hut. Eight students, three of them Americans, spent two hours, twice a week taking skeletons apart and hacking cadavers to pieces. The huts were not air-conditioned, and they lacked windows. It got hot inside those buildings. Sometimes you felt like you might suffocate.

"One day," Doug said, "we're in there sweating our asses off, working on this huge skeleton. I mean this son of a bitch was just made for the NBA. Must have been six-eight, six-nine—the biggest goddam Venezuelan in history. Perez struts around, tapping the skeleton with his pointer, putting on a show, basically saying stuff about as smart as *the knee bone's connected to the thigh bone.*

"After about four hours, we've got that son of a bitch completely disassembled, all of the bones piled up on one big table. Normally you'd take a skeleton apart one class and put it back together the next. All of us are thinking thank God, we can get some air now, when Perez says to one guy, 'Okay. Now count the bones.'"

Keep in mind that a hot tub is not a particularly large vessel. Ours was smaller than most. Doug Hench and I were jammed in knee to knee, toe to toe. The quarters were anything but spacious, yet strangely enough I didn't feel cramped. A cloud of steam hung in the air, and the night was quiet except for our voices and the sloshing sound the water made when one of us shifted position. I felt loose and relaxed. Peaceful.

I felt close to Doug Hench. The closeness was not purely the result of physical proximity. The closeness, I can see now, came from an awareness that Doug Hench saw the narrative possibilities his own life offered. And I must have understood already that like me, Doug Hench was not the sole author of the story that he was. Somebody else shared the copyright and received the royalty statements. And whoever that individual was, he knew one thing well: Doug Hench was not a best-seller.

"What happened," I said, "when they counted the bones?"

"One bone was gone. Perez got out the loose-leaf binder that contained what he called his bone catalog, and he made us check off the bones, one at a time. The atlas bone was missing. It's the first cervical vertebra of the neck—it's actually what supports the head."

Doug said Perez walked over to the door and pulled out a key and locked it. Though everyone else was soaking wet by that time, Perez's own shirt was dry.

Perez looked cool, and when he spoke his voice was

icy. "Someone," he said, "has stolen the bone. The thief is among us. He has committed an act of desecration. Not only he is unfit to serve in the medical profession, he is unfit to breathe and walk the Earth. And so until he produces the bone, he will not walk the Earth, and in a short time, I think it's fair to say, he will have great difficulty breathing. No one leaves this building until the bone is in my hand."

Perez hit a switch, and the lights went out. "The thief," he said, "has exactly sixty seconds to lay the bone on the table."

They waited there in the suffocating darkness. Doug began to feel guilty, as if he were the one who had stolen the bone. He felt as if it were his responsibility to produce it, even though he didn't have it. And then, as little rivulets of sweat ran down his spine, he began to fear that he did have it, that it was somewhere on his person and in the end would be discovered. If that happened, he decided, he would not go home. He would offer his own body to science.

Perez hit the light switch. The table was bare.

He walked back over to the door and inserted his key. "Gentlemen," he said, "the *guardia* will keep you company. For all practical purposes, you are under arrest."

Doug scooped up some water and sloshed it on his chest. Trudi's breasts were formidable, but nothing compared to Doug's. They were huge and white, real cellulite marvels. You had to wonder what he'd look like when he turned sixty. You had to wonder, given his present size and his shortness of breath, if he would turn sixty.

"The thing is," Doug said, "there was another way out. All of us knew it, and so did Perez."

"Another door?"

"Not that kind of way out. What I mean is, quite a few medical students down there, especially the foreigners, owned their own skeletons. I had one myself."

It was Venezuela, Doug said. The groundskeepers at many cemeteries were poor first, Catholic second. If you found the right one and laid enough money on him, he could generally get you a skeleton in good condition. You could hang it in your closet, Doug said, and get a leg up on the anatomy class.

Doug was elected to negotiate. The *guardia*—there were two of them who patrolled the campus, both packing sidearms—escorted him to Perez's office. Perez listened to his plea, then agreed to let everybody out of the building.

"You've got until eight in the morning to produce that bone," he told Doug. "If I don't have it then, I'll file charges. And Hench?"

Doug had turned to go. When he looked back at Perez, it struck him that Perez, despite the difference in skin color, bore a certain resemblance to his own father. They weren't the same size, but they exhibited a similarity in bearing. There was something militaristic about their behavior toward him. They saw him, he felt, as a wayward private, the kind of guy who'd fall down as soon as you said *March*.

"You might have noticed that the gentleman whose

substructure we were working on was by no means a midget," Perez said. "Probably not elephantine like you, since his bones don't show the kind of deterioration you'd normally find in obese people, but he was a big man. That bone, *Señor,* had better be the right size."

As I have said, Doug Hench was drunk when he showed up that night, and at dinner he'd gotten even drunker. But the story he was telling affected him like a strong cup of coffee. He'd sobered up. He was beginning to make a run at profundity.

"When you start dealing with the body," he said, "you realize how individual each and every one of us is—you can't hang one man's flesh on another man's bones. I may be grotesque, I may share a lot of physical traits with other grotesque people, but by God there's only one Doug Hench."

And there had only been one of whomever the missing atlas bone belonged to. No matter what bone Doug Hench and company found, it would not fit the skeleton perfectly. The best they could hope to do was find one that looked right, then pray that it satisfied Perez.

A second-year student from Florida had a tall skeleton—he kept it disassembled in the trunk of his Audi— but he refused to sell the atlas bone. A couple of other students were willing to sell, but upon examination their bones proved too small.

Around midnight, one of the Venezuelan students burst into the apartment Doug shared with another American and announced that he had located an atlas bone that would most likely do. The problem was that the student who owned it knew what a mess they were in, and he intended to milk them dry. He was asking five hundred dollars.

Somehow the eight of them got it together. The Venezuelan student who'd found the bone went and put down a deposit on it, brought it back for the rest of them to look at, had it approved, then returned to pay the owner the remainder of the five hundred dollars.

For whatever reason, Doug had achieved a certain stature among the other students at the institute. After all, they'd chosen him to negotiate with Perez, and the negotiations had led to this happy resolution. Nobody would be expelled, nobody would go to jail. Everybody, thanks to Doug, could still look forward to the day when he could call himself *doctor.*

And so, at two A.M., the bone was left with Doug for safekeeping.

"And that," said Doug, "should have been the end of the story."

If that had been the end of that story, this story would now be ending as well. Doug Hench and I would emerge from the hot tub, steam rising off our bodies, Doug hairy and humongous, prehistoric-looking, a big cave man surrounded by the primeval mist, me a lot smaller, more modern in appearance, maybe, but clearly of the same species.

We would dry ourselves off, put on our clothes, shake hands like good neighbors, and bid each other goodnight. I would go to my wife, and Doug would go to his. I would be asked to explain myself, to make Trudi understand why, having been gone for the better part of five months, I had now chosen to sit in the hot tub until well past midnight, with a man who reminded her of the horrific Hermann Göring.

Doug, I suspect, would not have been asked to explain himself. Araceli already knew who he was and what he was about. Many people, it occurred to me, would look at Doug and think they knew what he was about. They would think that Doug was about appetite. These same people, looking at me, would see my uniform and think they knew what I was about too. I was about destruction. I was about bombs and missiles and kill-counts. I was Texaco's techno-cowpoke, the man who cracked the whip on the mavericks.

The great irony was that Doug had taken human life and I had not. He had taken it for the best of reasons, to end suffering, and I had failed to take it for the worst: because no opportunity had presented itself.

"My roommate," Doug said, "had this great big Afghan hound."

Theft is so disturbing because it's unforseen. One day you're driving down the street listening to Brahms on the CD player, the next day you walk into the driveway to find a pile of glass lying near the car. You look through the shattered window, see the hole in the dashboard where the Sony used to be and you feel helpless, violated. You phone the insurance company, pay the deductible, lock the car up at night in the garage. You're out a hundred dollars, and you find yourself wondering if death comes like that, so swift, so sudden, so eager to leave a hole in the dash.

Doug had wrapped the atlas bone in a washcloth and left it lying on the counter in the kitchen. When he walked into the kitchen the next morning, the washcloth was on the floor. The Afghan, whose name was Honey, lay asleep near the refrigerator.

Doug poked her with his foot. "Hey!" he said. "Honey!"

She sat up.

"Did you eat my damn bone?"

Honey yawned. Then she licked her chops.

Perez stood behind his desk. He wore a black suit and a black tie. His face was grim. He looked, Doug said, as if he were bound for a funeral. Or an execution.

"Hench," he said, "where's my bone?"

"There's this cliché we have in universities in the U.S.," Doug said. He was sweating badly. His shirt was plastered to his back. The other seven students were waiting outside in the anteroom. Earlier, when he'd told them what had happened to the bone, one of them had grabbed his shirt collar and ripped it. He stood there now with his collar open, the front of his soaking shirt tattered. He was exactly where his father had predicted he would be. In disgrace. But even his father could not have guessed he would be undone by an Afghan hound. "The cliché," he said, "is that when a student doesn't write his paper, he goes in and tells the professor *My dog ate it.*"

"Hench," Perez said.

"My dog didn't eat it," Doug said, "but my roommate's dog did."

Perez did not explode. The muscles in his face actually relaxed. "Very well," he said. He walked around the desk and opened the door to his outer office. He stood aside, gestured for Doug to step out into the anteroom, then he followed him.

Perez crossed his arms. "Gentlemen," he said, "I suggest that each of you make every effort to get as far away from the institute as is humanly possibly, and I suggest you begin your efforts right now. I intend to pick up the phone when I return to my office. I'm going to charge all of you with theft of human remains, which, in case you didn't know it, can keep you in jail until you're nothing more than remains yourselves. I bid each and every one of you a heartfelt goodbye."

Imagine the self-loathing.

Imagine, if you can, going home to tell your father that an Afghan hound had turned you into a fugitive from justice.

Imagine, if you can, telling him that terminal ineptness, an inability to avoid unfavorable circumstances, had made it impossible for you to assume his title, wear his mantle, bear his crest into the next century, hand it on.

Imagine the dusty hotel room in Caracas where, fearing arrest, Doug Hench sought refuge. The dust assaulted his nasal passages, made him sneeze and cough. As always when he felt frightened, he gorged. He ate bad meat for dinner, a lot of it, followed by three bowls of ice cream. He woke up poisoned. He vomited, had diarrhea every four or five minutes. His fever soared, chills racked his body, he hugged himself and cried. He wept for all that he was and all that he was not. In his delirium, he prayed that his father would appear in the room to administer an injection, lethal or curative, it did not matter which, so long as his suffering ceased.

Which, in due course, it did. And at the end of five days, some twenty pounds lighter, purged of a certain portion of himself, Doug Hench appeared at eight o'clock sharp in the office of his accuser, Dr. Alejandro Perez, Professor of Medicine, purported author of *Perez's Anatomy,* and said to him, "Here I am, sir. You can turn me in."

It would make a more moving scene if Perez smiled, if his lip curled mischievously, or, better yet, if a few tears appeared in his steely gray eyes. He could have said a line or two about the magic of the moment when the boy becomes the man. But none of these things happened. His face betrayed no emotion whatsoever as he assayed this lighter, combat-ready, take-it-in-the-chest version of North American Doug.

"There are four of you now," Perez said. "Class starts in fifteen minutes."

It was late. We climbed from the tub, the steam rising from our bodies, and began to towel off. Doug stood there beside me, ghostly white, outflanked by his own hips. He bent to slip on his shorts, and as he did so, I pointed out that he still hadn't answered my question. He

hadn't said why he did what he did—why he continued
to practice medicine, even though his practice was a poor
one and he hated the work.

I believed, as by now you surely must, that he would
say he did it because his father had expected him to do it.
I believed that he had failed to say so, in so many words,
because he thought the story illustrated the point well
enough. It had shown that in the name of our fathers and
the service of their causes we commit acts of profanation
and desecration, that the fathers are everywhere among
us and in this life you can never escape them, because
when you leave one behind, another will turn up. In the
end we ourselves become the fathers, and so there is not
and cannot be among men such a thing as brotherhood,
only fatherhood and sonhood, and the only just act is to
annihilate the father in ourselves. Patricide begins at
home.

Standing there, bare to the waist, Doug Hench glanced
over the fence, at his own house, where his wife, Araceli,
lay sleeping. He sighed and pulled on his filthy T-shirt.
Without saying another word, he trudged across the
yard, through the gate, and into the night.

Angel, Hold Your Horses

"KATIE?" UNCLE Billy said. "Honey, are you awake?"

I hadn't been until he spoke, but now I was. Not just awake, but wide awake. It was a skill I'd learned, how to be sound asleep one second, then alert the next. It's something I can still do today.

"Yeah," I said.

Uncle Billy was in his mid-thirties then, but his hair had already turned gray. Except for that, he looked exactly like my father had looked. He had a pleasant enough face, nice blue eyes. At various times in their lives he and Daddy had been mistaken for one another. Once, after a high school dance, they'd switched places and fooled their dates. Daddy used to brag about that.

"We're almost there," Uncle Billy said. He glanced past me at Walter.

My brother's head rested against the window glass. His eyes were shut tight. His hands had balled themselves up into fists. He always slept like that, like he was ready for a

fight. But he wasn't like me. It took a lot of doing to wake
him up.

The wipers hurled sheets of water off the windshield.
It had been raining hard when we left Jackson, and it was
raining hard now. The road was slick.

It was a one-lane blacktop that ran between two cotton
fields. It looked like any other road in the Delta, I guess,
but it pleased me to think I recognized it. I hadn't been
here in more than four years. A lot had changed in that
time, but the road hadn't, it was still the same strip of asphalt it had been way back then.

Aunt Margaret's house stood right at the edge of a
field. It was a farmhouse, a small one with white shingles
on the sides and brown shingles on the roof, but Aunt
Margaret didn't farm. She was the bookkeeper at Delta
Implement in Indianola. Her husband had been the
farmer. He'd left her a year or two ago. As I understood it,
nobody knew where he was.

"Maybe Lula's run off to be with Larry," Aunt Dot had
said in the kitchen last night. "Maybe if you find her,
you'll find him too."

Aunt Dot was Uncle Billy's wife. Lula was my mother,
Larry was Aunt Margaret's husband, the man who'd run
off. Aunt Margaret and Uncle Billy were my dead father's
sister and brother.

It gets confusing, I know. All these names, all these
family relationships. I'd like to say just forget all the ones
that were dead or missing, I'd like to tell you they're not
important to the story, but the truth is they may be the
most important of all.

Them and Matt. He was standing there on the porch
that morning with Aunt Margaret, both of them waiting,

watching for us to show. He was already tall as his momma, and Aunt Margaret was not a short lady.

We ran across the yard jumping puddles, dodging a skinny dog that came tearing out from under the porch, barking like he meant to rip our hides.

"Shut up," Matt yelled at the dog. "You damned old mongrel. Don't nobody know where you come from."

He bent and grabbed a rock from a pile that lay on the porch and then he straightened up and drew his arm back. The dog meant to bite me, I knew he did, but the look on Matt's face made me feel for the animal. Matt hurled the rock sidearmed. It thudded against the dog, who howled and ran back under the house.

"Did you see that?" Walter said later, after we'd gone inside and dried off. My brother loved animals, had loved them all his life. He was twelve years old and had never owned a dog or a cat or a pet of any kind, but all the animals on our street had been as much his as anybody else's. Two or three neighborhood dogs had always followed him to school. "Anybody that'd do that to a dog," Walter said, shaking his head, "hell, there ain't no telling about him. There flat ain't no telling."

We had come to Indianola to stay with Aunt Margaret because the previous day, a Monday, our momma had left us. It had been the first day of summer vacation. I'd woken up right around seven o'clock, just like I would have if school had been in session, and I'd put on my bathrobe and walked down the hall to the kitchen. It would take me a week or so, I figured, to get used to sleeping longer.

Momma had a job checking groceries at the Jitney-Jungle on West Capitol, and she was supposed to be at work by eight-thirty. I expected her to be in the kitchen, drinking coffee, possibly talking to some man I'd never seen before, who would more than likely be wearing Daddy's old bathrobe. But that morning nobody was there.

All the dishes had been washed and stacked in the dish rack. The drying rag was still damp. A note lay on the table. It said *You all call your Uncle Billy. He'll take care of you or see to it somebody does. I'm sorry. I hope you'll one day forgive me. Momma.*

I can't say I've never walked out on anybody, because I have. But everybody I've ever walked out on was grown, and I never did it while they were asleep. Every time I left, I looked the person I was leaving right straight in the eye. It didn't matter whether I was taking off due to something silly, like him neglecting to wash his dishes till finally I came to think of him as nothing more than a gravy-stained bowl, or whether I'd caught him in the sack, like I did one time, with my next-door neighbor. I'm going, I said. Here's why.

But the morning Momma left, it was that sheet of paper that told me, and ever since then the sight of a piece of white paper lying on a table or a countertop has made me weak in the knees.

I walked back down the hall and into the room I shared with Walter. It was a tiny room, just barely big enough to hold our bunk bed. There were ugly brown stains on the ceiling. We'd dealt with a lot of bad news in that room, and the truth was I hated it. But at least I knew how to deal with bad news there. Dealing with bad news elsewhere was something I might have to work on.

I put my hand on Walter's shoulder and shook him. He didn't budge. I shook him again.

"Wake up," I said.

He finally opened his eyes.

"Momma's gone," I said.

It tells you something about our family, I guess, that Walter never once thought I meant Momma had gone to work. He knew I meant gone in the big sense. But even in the big sense, there are different kinds of gone.

He sat up. "Dead?" he said. "Or in the road?"

"In the road," I said, because that was all I could swear to.

I called Aunt Dot and gave her the news in a matter-of-fact way, like it was no big deal. I must have understood that we were about to become objects of pity and that the disadvantages of being pitied far outweighed the advantages. "Momma's left us," I said. "The note said to call y'all."

"Jesus," she said. "The good Lord didn't want the world to be boring, so He cooked up the likes of Lula."

She called Uncle Billy at the pesticide company where he worked, and he came for us in his pickup truck. For some reason, he and Dot seemed to think we needed to go to bed, even though it was just mid-morning and we'd been asleep for eight or ten hours. They sent their kids—they had a house full of them—out to the park to play, and Dot stripped the sheets off two beds and put clean ones on and kept saying "Y'all must be exhausted, you just need to rest."

It had been like that the day Daddy died. It was summertime then too, and Momma had left us at home alone, hooked up to the television set while she went out to buy groceries. Aunt Dot was the one who showed up to break the news. She'd knocked on the door in the middle of the day, her eyes red-rimmed, and she'd headed straight for our bedroom and started turning back the covers on our beds, saying something about Eagle Lake, about Daddy and Uncle Billy going fishing in a boat, and then something about Uncle Billy turning his back.

"He just turned his back," she'd said. She fluffed my lumpy old pillow. "Just for a minute, a second, he turned his back, and then he turned around. And children, your daddy was gone."

Our daddy was not above playing practical jokes on other adults. Once, I knew, he'd parked his pickup truck on another street and hidden in the hall closet and then jumped out and said *Boo* to Momma. He'd told us all about it at the supper table. "Your momma," he said, "looked like she'd seen a ghost."

"He's probably just playing a trick," I told Aunt Dot. "He's probably just trying to fool Uncle Billy."

"Oh, honey," she said. "They're dragging the lake."

"What's that mean?"

"Baby, they're trying to pull up his body."

The distance between her last two words was what froze me. Daddy was now one thing, and his body was another.

"Y'all get in bed," she said. She nudged Walter toward the lower bunk. He crawled in, and she pulled the covers up to his neck and tucked him in.

I must have climbed into the upper bunk because the next thing I knew she was tucking me in too. I lay there above my brother, staring at the brown stains on the ceiling, knowing they'd been left there by water.

Aunt Margaret acted calm, like it truly was no big deal that Momma had run off. Aunt Margaret had been deserted herself, and in the years since all of this happened, I've come to believe that you can divide people up on the basis of whether or not they've ever been abandoned. You can take things a step further and divide up those who have according to when and how they were left. Uncle Larry, so Matt would tell me a little later that summer, had left in the middle of the night, just like Momma. He'd left after a fight, during which he told Aunt Margaret that she'd kept her ass in cold storage so long it had turned to dry ice. I imagine that after hearing that from the father of her son, she'd grown a little bit numb.

Our first morning at her place she got up early to fix breakfast. I was sleeping on the living room couch by myself—she'd put an army cot in Matt's room for Walter to sleep on—and I lay there awake that morning, listening to her cook. While she moved around the kitchen, scrambling eggs and frying bacon, she hummed softly, one hymn blending with another. "Just as I Am" became "Standing on the Promises," and that one ran right into "Love Lifted Me."

At breakfast you could tell Matt and Walter hadn't gotten along especially well during the night. "Can I have some butter?" Walter said.

Matt was fourteen, a year older than me. He had
a square jaw, a dimple in his chin, coal black hair, and
eyes so dark that they suggested pure absence. Whoever
Momma had left for, I figured, stood a fair chance of
being an older version of Matt.

He picked up the butter dish and kind of jabbed it at
Walter. "Here, Johnny U."

Walter's face darkened. "Never mind."

"Suit yourself," Matt said. He set the butter dish back
down.

Aunt Margaret sipped her coffee. "What's this all
about?"

"He's trying to convince me the only decent football
in the state's played in the Big Eight," Matt said. "He
thinks the Delta Valley Conference is just a kindergarten
league."

"That ain't what I said."

"What did you say?"

"What he said don't matter," Aunt Margaret said.
"What matters is that Walter's a guest here, Matt, and it's
up to you to make him feel welcome."

Matt ducked his head. He was still at the stage where
he had to pretend to show respect for his momma,
though later on it became clear to me that he didn't respect her at all. He didn't respect her because the way
he saw it, it had been up to her to keep his daddy at
home, and somehow she'd failed at the only task that
mattered.

After breakfast she told us it'd be our job to wash the
dishes every morning and we'd have to fix our own
lunch. Walter and Matt would get together on taking care
of the yard, and I was responsible for cleaning the house.

She was sorry, she said, about what had happened, but things would work out somehow, and in the meantime it was going to be a huge help to her to have us around.

She left for town, and there we were. For a while the three of us sat on the porch, Matt and Walter not even looking at one another. But every now and then Matt glanced at me. I knew what he was thinking about.

He was thinking about that day four years ago when I'd walked out into the woods behind the house with him. We'd played in those woods, on weekends when we came to visit. We'd played Robin Hood in them, played cowboys and Indians, played GI's and Germans. But that day four years ago Matt said he didn't want to play. He said he wanted me to watch him do something. And I stood there, my back against the bark of a tree, while he did what he had to do.

I didn't bother to wonder why he wanted to do it in front of me. It seemed like a natural enough thing. I'd already seen two boys do it, a pair of twins that lived on our street. A drainage ditch cut our block in two, and there was a big culvert that ran under the pavement. The twins had done it in there while I watched, and that time it had scared me. I'd gone home and told Momma. I remember she was shelling purple-hulled peas at the time, watching TV. She was wearing tight shorts and a white bra. We didn't have an air conditioner, and the house was stifling. Her skin was shiny from sweat.

She sat her pan down and took my hand. "Boys just need to do that," she said. "As long as they're doing that and nothing else, I wouldn't worry."

"But why do they want me to watch?"

"Well, they're at a stage right now," she said, "where

they kind of like an audience." She let go of my hand and picked up her pan, and it seemed like she'd said all she aimed to say. But as I turned away, she spoke again. "Actually," she said, "the stage the twins are at is the least dangerous stage of all."

As the three of us sat there on Aunt Margaret's porch that morning, I knew full well that Matt had progressed to a lot more dangerous stage. But for some reason that I couldn't have explained, I believed he was more dangerous to my brother than he could ever be to me.

"Well," he finally said, "I don't aim to just sit here all day. Can you hit a baseball, Johnny U, or do the NFL rules limit you to football?"

Walter was sitting in a lawn chair. His fingers closed around the metal armrests, squeezing them. I remember thinking that he had a lot to prove. Unless Uncle Billy found Momma or she came back pretty quick on her own, Walter was in for a long summer, three months of being dogged from within and without. All I'd have to deal with, I thought, was the empty hole in the middle of my chest, that absence I didn't know a name for. It seemed, right then, like I'd got the better deal.

A big white propane tank stood in one corner of the yard. They used it as a backstop that morning. Matt started out as the pitcher, and while I sat there watching he hurled one pitch after another past Walter, who flailed at the ball so hard he lost his balance once or twice and went down in the mud. He tore the knees out of his jeans. A big brown stain spread across his seat, making it look like he'd soiled himself.

Ball after ball thumped the tank, Walter's bat whisked

the air. Every third time my brother missed, Matt raised his fist and hollered "K" and glanced my way.

Finally I decided to try an experiment. Without saying anything, I got up off the porch and went inside. I walked over to the window, crouched down, and lifted up the edge of the curtain. Matt was staring at the porch, at the empty lawn chair where I'd been sitting.

"Hell," he said. He tossed his glove toward the house, as if in disgust. "I can't play with you, Johnny U. You blind or what?"

Walter let the bat dangle by his leg for a few seconds, then he dropped it on the ground. He didn't drop it in any angry sort of way, it wasn't like the way Matt had thrown the glove. The bat hadn't failed Walter, Walter had failed the bat. You could tell he was thinking that.

"No, I'm not blind," he said, his voice tinged with regret.

You know how when you're having money trouble, you can put it out of your mind and put it out of your mind, just thinking that somehow, surely, something's going to come along and solve your problems—that you'll win a grocery store jackpot or you'll just be walking along one day and there'll be an envelope in the ditch with five thousand dollars inside it? You think like that and think like that until one day a collection agency calls and you can't hide from the problems anymore, and suddenly your troubles seem about twelve times worse than you ever thought they could be.

That's what it was like that summer for Walter and me. In the back of our minds we really thought we wouldn't be at Aunt Margaret's too long. We thought our problem, our worst one anyway, would soon be solved. Uncle Billy had claimed he'd find Momma, and we believed in Uncle Billy. We'd always believed in Uncle Billy, in ways that we'd never believed in our own daddy.

Our daddy had been the kind of man who loved to give his kids things—he bought us candy on his way home from work and hollered *time for sweets* when he walked in, and every week or two he bought us small toys, dump trucks and water pistols for Walter, dolls and crayons for me—but he hadn't liked to spend time playing with us, and it's in play that kids start to trust adults. Nine times out of ten, when I got an image of Daddy in my mind, a newspaper was hiding his face. He'd sold tires for a living at a Firestone service center down the street from Livingston Park Zoo, and when he came home every afternoon, he brought the *Jackson Daily* with him and spent an hour or two behind it. If I asked him to draw with me or read me a book, he'd always say "Angel, hold your horses" and go right back to reading the paper, and if Walter asked him to go out and throw a ball, he'd say "Maybe later," but later it would be dark.

Uncle Billy had always had time for both of us, and Uncle Billy was often around. Even before Daddy drowned, we got used to coming home from school and finding Uncle Billy's truck parked at the curb. He fixed things around our house, things Daddy wouldn't touch, like the stove and the washing machine and, even once, our TV. But when we got home, he'd drop whatever he was doing and spend a few minutes playing with us, while Momma moved around in the kitchen fixing supper. I'd let him throw me into the air, and so would Walter, and if he'd told me to jump off the house, I probably would have done it, because if Uncle Billy said do it, it just couldn't hurt. So when he said he'd find Momma and told us not to worry, we didn't.

A couple of weeks passed. We didn't see him and we didn't see her. And then, all at once, it hit us. Hard.

I was in the house, mopping the kitchen floor, when I heard the sound of shattering glass. I ran into the hallway. The bathroom door was open, and shards of glass lay all over the tiles in front of the toilet. In the middle of the floor was a golf ball.

I stepped over the glass and looked through the broken windowpane. Walter was standing in the yard, the brim of a green baseball cap pulled down over his eyes. The bat lay at his feet.

"What did you do?"

"I'm trying to learn how to hit."

"A golf ball?"

"If you can hit one of them, you sure as hell ought to be able to hit a baseball."

"Why did you hit it toward the house?"

He shrugged. "Hooked it."

Matt had gone to town that morning with Aunt Margaret, to spend the day playing baseball with some kids from his school. She'd made him invite Walter, but Walter had said no thanks. Matt hadn't let up on Walter that much in the last two weeks, though there were days when he gave up deviling him long enough to spend some time watching me. He'd follow me around the house while I did the cleaning. He never offered to help, but every now and then he'd say "Look over yonder in the corner, seem like you missed a spot." He'd do anything he could to make me bend over. He didn't care whether he was in front of me or behind me when I did it, just so long as he was standing somewhere nearby.

I started to tell Walter he'd better be glad we were here by ourselves, since Matt would have embarrassed him to death if he'd been around to witness the accident. Then it occurred to me that it might not matter much whether or not Matt had seen it. The windowpane was broken, and there wasn't a thing in the world we could do about that. When Aunt Margaret got home, we'd have to tell her.

But we didn't have to tell her the complete truth. I'd lived my whole life in a world full of lies, though I didn't know it at that moment. All I knew was that I aimed to tell one.

"Listen," I said, "you get in here and help me clean this up."

He came in and while I swept the glass up into a neat pile, he squatted, holding Aunt Margaret's metal dustpan. I swept the glass into it, and then I said, "You know how this happened?"

He tipped the brim of his cap back, so that I could see his eyes. "How?"

"I was in here mopping the tiles," I said, "and I slipped, and when I slipped I kind of threw the mop out behind me, and the handle hit the windowpane and smashed it."

He squatted there before me, looking up at me, that panful of broken glass in his hand. "It's just us, ain't it?"

he said. "Uncle Billy's not gonna find Momma. She's not coming back."

"I don't think she is," I said.

As it turned out, time would prove both of us wrong. Figured in the ordinary way, it wouldn't even be that long before it happened. One day in the first week of August, we'd see a truck coming toward us on the blacktop road. As it got closer, the truck would become a red truck, then it would become a red truck with white door panels and CB antenna, and Walter would say, "It's Uncle Billy."

The truck would pull up beside Aunt Margaret's mailbox, and Momma would get out. She'd be wearing a pair of red pants that were too tight for her and a white T-shirt with a coffee stain on it. She'd walk across the grass, toward me and Walter, and when she got close, we'd see the glaze on her cheeks and the red streaks in her eyes, and before she managed a word, Walter and I would be up and moving into her arms.

But I didn't count time in the ordinary way. When Daddy drowned, I'd learned to measure time in my own personal way. The way I counted time, a year could wind up having no significance, but a second could make all the difference in the world. There are instants when ages roll. That summer at Aunt Margaret's, Walter and I became old.

For the Fourth of July, Aunt Margaret planned a party. The party would just be for the four of us. She talked about it for at least ten days beforehand, making plans, going on about the homemade ice cream we'd eat, about

the way the fireworks she'd bought across the river in
Arkansas would light up the night sky. It wasn't her
favorite holiday, she said, Christmas was number one,
but the Fourth was probably number two.

"You know what we used to do?" she said. It was
suppertime, the night before the Fourth. "We used to go
over to Greenville and rent a motorboat at the Marina
and get out on Lake Fergusson and ski. Can you imagine
that?" she said. "Me?"

What she meant was could we imagine somebody her
size, with her build, skimming across the water in a
bathing suit. "I bet you did it real good," I said.

"No, she didn't," Matt said. "She had trouble getting
up. Daddy dragged her halfway across the lake one day
with her head in the water. He like to. . . ."

His voice trailed off. Even Matt was sensitive enough to
know that *drag* and *lake* were not words you wanted to
use in our presence.

After supper, it being Wednesday night, Aunt Margaret got dressed up and went to prayer meeting. I'd
taken to going out and walking down the road sometimes
right around dusk, and I took a notion to do it that night.
I was preparing myself, I can see now, for an independent
life, getting ready to be alone in the dark.

It was a cooler night than we'd been having. Katydids
sang their dry chorus; a soft breeze rustled the leaves on
the cotton.

The cotton was dark green and about three feet tall
right then. Tall enough for somebody who wanted to
conceal himself while keeping pace with you. If somebody had wanted to do that, he would have bent real low
and crept along between two rows fifteen or twenty yards

from the road. And then, when it was almost dark and you were a mile from the house, way out in the middle of the country, where the next car or truck might not come along for another hour or two, he'd hunker down there in the field and make a sound he thought you'd associate with ghosts and haunted houses—*wooooooooooo!*—and after that he'd wait to see if he'd scared you.

He couldn't know that there were times when you longed to see a ghost, that while many things did frighten you, an encounter with the dead was not among them. He didn't know that no sound could scare you, that an absence of sound was the thing you feared, or that it was this fear that made you walk alone at night, that you were steeping yourself in silence.

I crossed my arms and looked his way. He grinned and came toward me, parting the thick stands of cotton with his forearms, stepping over the rows and then jumping the road ditch.

"Hey," he said.

"Hey."

"I shouldn't have said that about dragging momma through the lake. I'm sorry. As far as that goes, I shouldn't have tried to scare you right now. I'm sorry about that too. I did it because I'm a little scared myself."

All my life, I've had a problem when males apologize to me. It doesn't happen that often, but when it does my natural tendency is to want to forgive anything they've done. I forgive and forgive until the forgiveness well runs dry, and then I get in the road.

The first time a guy apologized to me was the time I just told about now. I was standing in the road when it happened, and it's a shame I didn't just keep walking.

"What are you scared of?" I said.

"You know."

"I don't have any idea."

He jammed his hands into his pockets. He glanced back down the road, toward the house. And in that instant, I have to say, he really did look scared.

The condition of the pavement suddenly seemed to enthrall him. "You," he said.

"Me?"

"What you might say. Who you might say it to."

"Say what? About what?"

"You know," he said again.

I did know, but I didn't aim to say so. If it was going to be put into words, he'd have to do the putting. "No," I said, "I don't know."

"That time you watched me."

I don't remember moving my feet, and maybe I didn't. Yet I had the impression that we'd just come closer to one another. In my memory, his face is inches from mine. I can hear his breath, see the faint fuzz on his cheeks. His eyes are big and round.

"What about it?"

"How would you feel," he said, "if I'd watched you do something like that?"

"I don't know," I said.

He told me later it was almost like I was asking him to do what he did next. That's always the way, isn't it? Where there's no question mark they hear one, where there's no invitation they read *RSVP*.

He put both arms around me. When he pressed his mouth to mine, sound filled my ears, a puzzling sound, one I couldn't account for until later, when I understood that a heart can roar just as well as beat and pound.

Matt's daddy, Uncle Larry, had raised cattle at one time, just a few of them, Matt said. "It was like everything else he tried to do," Matt said. "It didn't come to much. About the only thing he ever did well was run off."

The wooden shed he'd kept the feed in was still standing. It was behind the house, on the far side of the barn. The first time I went in it, that same night Matt stopped me on the road, I noticed an odd smell in the air.

"What's that odor?"

"Cottonseed meal and cottonseed hulls."

"I thought cows ate hay."

"They do. But come wintertime you feed 'em extra stuff too—if you want 'em to give milk."

The word *milk* hung in the air between us. Reaching for me in the darkness, pushing up my shirt to rub my breasts too hard, he made a sound that was not far from a sob.

"Katie," he said, "please please please."

The floorboards were rough and uneven, and when I sank onto them, they felt spongy, like the floor might give way. "Wait," he said, and he spread an empty feed sack for me to lay back on.

That was the first time, with that burlap sack pressed against my back, making me itch, those floorboards creaking and groaning and then another sort of groaning, this big sound coming from somewhere, from me, from someplace in me deeper than my throat, deeper than my diaphragm even. The sound filled the shed; it was so loud I was convinced they could hear it in town.

It was dark in there, but my eyes had adjusted, and I could see my own feet in the air. I didn't know how they'd got up there. Feet didn't belong in the air. My toes splayed out tense and rigid.

I'm not saying I loved it, but I'm not saying I didn't learn to like it. What I'm saying is, this is what passed between us that summer. Several nights I went to the feed shed, and I didn't go alone.

You could kind of feel it coming from the early morning on. On days when he aimed to ask me to go to the shed with him, Matt would hang around the kitchen, he'd help me wash dishes, he'd dry them and stack them in the cabinet. If Walter tried to help, Matt would say, "Aw, hell, Walter, you're company. Go on out there and play. Hit some fly balls, why don't you, and in a minute or two I'll come out and pitch you a few."

At first, Walter's face would go slack when Matt acted nice toward him, but in no time he began to buy it.

"He's not so bad," Walter said. "Me and him might could be buddies."

Matt quit throwing balls past him, he eased up on his pitches, let Walter lay the bat on the ball.

"You're getting the knack of it," Matt would say when Walter knocked one into the field across the road. "Hey, that's the way."

It was not as long as you might think before I understood that whatever else might come of it, one product of my going to the feed shed with Matt was a little bit of peace for my brother. And once I understood that,

I couldn't refuse to go, even if I'd wanted to. Which I didn't.

There are two kinds of knowing.

There's the kind that comes sudden, where the big question is answered all at once and it's a while before the little ones start to nag you. Your daddy's dead, that's the big thing. It's three days till they find his body, it's a year before you hear a neighbor ask your momma what she thinks made the gash in his forehead, and your momma says maybe the propeller. It's a little while longer till you wonder about that, and it nags you a day or two and then you forget.

There's the kind that comes slow, where the facts add up day by day, week by week. Your sister disappears from the house around the same time most nights. You see her head off down the road, you watch her till she's almost out of sight. Your cousin puts on his shorts and says he's going to jog, that he's got to get in shape for fall and football, but he never invites you to come along, even though you know he can run you in the ground, and you can't figure out why he wouldn't get a kick out of doing it. Then you finally say it to yourself. In the end this kind of knowing is sort of sudden too, because there's that single instant when you admit possessing knowledge.

I watched it happen. From the window I watched the first of it, the same bathroom window Walter had knocked the ball through. It happened on a Monday morning right toward the end of July, not too long after

Aunt Margaret left for work. We didn't know it then, but Momma would show up within a week, her and Uncle Billy would ride up one day, and in less than an hour we'd all be on our way back to Jackson. We'd take up where we'd left off, more or less. We'd move back into the same house, Momma would go to work at another grocery store. In a few years I'd graduate from high school, Walter would leave to join the marines, and a year after that he'd die in a bunker at Khe Sanh. They lined those bunkers, so I'm told, with sandbags made out of burlap.

I'd been in there using the bathroom. I'd just stood up and wiped myself when I looked out the window. Walter was out there holding the baseball bat. Matt stood before him. His baseball glove lay on the ground.

Walter drew the bat back and swung it at Matt's head, and Matt ducked and dove hard at Walter's knees. Walter went over backwards, and Matt began to beat him about the face.

I had my pants up then and was running, out the bathroom and down the hall and out the front door.

When I came around the corner of the house, I saw that they'd both regained their feet. Matt had Walter in a headlock, and he was dragging him over toward the road ditch.

"You think she don't want it?" I heard Matt say. "You think I made her? Man, you got the kind of momma men kill for. You think your sister's a nun, or what?"

It would be a few seconds before I started running again, before I threw myself at Matt, began to claw at his eyes and ears and draw as much blood as I could. For those few seconds I stood there and watched. From where I stood, Walter and Matt looked about the same size. Their hair was the same color, they had the same color eyes, they were both wearing blue jeans and T-shirts.

From where I stood, they could have passed for brothers, maybe even twins, and I'm sure that's what they would have looked like to you if you'd been driving by on the blacktop road that day. You might have wondered, as you sped by, headed toward town or wherever, why one of them was trying to push the other one head first into the road ditch, what lesson he believed the muddy stinking water might teach him.

The Warsaw Voice

"POLAND ISN'T what it used to be," I tell Anna.

We're walking through the woods toward Tama Brodzka, which is only worth going to because there's a bar between the railway station and the bus stop. It serves beer, warm and on tap. I'm a frequent customer these days.

Off to the right, where Lake Bachotek lies, you can hear the calls of wild ducks. This morning, as Anna and her mother and I sat on the pier, a formation flew over, necks outstretched, bills wide open. Watching them swoop down onto the water, maybe a half-mile away, I wondered aloud where they'd come from. Basia said, "You seem to be thinking a lot about origins."

"I am," I said. "Don't you ever do that?"

"I do," she said, staring through the mist at the wall of woods across the lake. "Now maybe more than ever."

It began raining a few minutes later, so we climbed the hill to the lake house. Anna sat at the table on the ground floor drawing, and Basia lay down on her bed. I switched on the electric radiator, sat down beside it, and read a few pages of Shelby Foote's Civil War trilogy. I've brought all three volumes with me—I reread them every few years—and this time around I'm halfway through the second. I'm taking my time. I don't know what I'll read when I finish the set. I'm trying not to think that far ahead.

"Our money's running out," Basia said, still lying on the bed.

"Toward the end at Vicksburg," I said, "Pemberton fed his soldiers saddle leather."

"This isn't Vicksburg," she said.

This isn't Vicksburg and my wife's not a historian. Otherwise she'd see that similarities abound.

The woods Anna and I are walking through are still wet. Rivulets run down the sleeves of her raincoat, which we bought on a Visa card the day before we left California. Her sneakers, I notice, look soggy.

"What did Poland used to be?" she asks me.

"You couldn't buy anything," I tell her.

"Can we buy things now?"

It's not a simple question, but I pretend it is. "Of course we can," I say. "Didn't we get those Legos down in Warsaw?"

"I thought we bought them in Warszawa."

Once, a couple of years ago, one of my former colleagues asked her if she was bilingual. "No," she said, "I'm Anna." She knows she's bilingual now, she accepts the fact that almost everything has at least two names that often sound nothing alike. But sometimes she has to be reminded.

After explaining that Warsaw and Warszawa are the same place, I tell her that the first time I came here, back in '85 when I met her mother, the stores were always empty, and usually there were long lines of people waiting out front.

"Why did they wait," she says, squeezing my hand, "if there wasn't anything they could buy?"

"They were waiting," I say, "because they kept hoping. They kept hoping something would turn up."

We break through the woods. Ten or twelve feet above us, beyond a metal guardrail, lies the highway to Torun. We walk along it for a few hundred yards. Cars whiz by. Some straddle the center line, others cut grooves along the shoulder. They're all doing about eighty-five or ninety. Some of the drivers have a full tank of gas for the first time in their lives, speed and power at the tips of their fingers.

Anna and I sit together at a table in the corner of the Universal Bar. A barmaid with the broad truculent face of a Polish peasant glares at us from time to time over the top of a translated Harlequin romance. Anna sips Pepsi, I drink beer. As usual, we're the only ones here. The place smells of cabbage, field sweat, and cigarettes.

"Daddy," Anna says when her bottle is empty, "why don't you tell me a story?"

She likes to hear them for the same reason I like to tell them: neither one of us knows how the tale will turn out.

"What kind?" I say.

"One about the guy who lived in Torun."

"The guy who learned the truth about the sun?"

"That's the one."

And so I tell her a story about Copernicus, whose green, dung-speckled statue she's seen standing before the town hall in Torun. "One night," I say, "Copernicus was taking a stroll along the Vistula. He was just a kid at the time, not too much older than you. A terrible disease had struck Torun. Back then, doctors didn't know some of the things they know now, and because they didn't, this disease had killed a lot of people. Copernicus's mother had just died, he himself had been sick, a lot of his playmates had died. He was trudging along without a destination—that means he didn't know where he was going. He just wanted to be close to the river. He wasn't looking at it, mind you, he was looking at the ground, but he could hear the water flowing, and he liked that rushing sound. It had been flowing for thousands of years, and it would be flowing when he went where his mother and his friends had gone.

"Suddenly, for some reason," I tell her, "he looked up into the heavens, and the night sky seemed to open up. He saw something big and round and incredibly bright. He just stood there gazing at it—it almost put his eyes out. Finally it vanished into nothing."

"It was the sun?" she says.

"No," I say. "Remember, this was at night."

"Maybe it was the moon."

"No, it wasn't that. He could see the moon too—this was something else."

"So what was it?"

"He never knew what it was," I tell her. "It might have been a cloud or it might have been dust or gas. Maybe it was nothing at all. Maybe he just imagined it."

"So what did he do?"

"What did he do?" I say, making a face as if I can't quite believe her question. "What do you think he did?"

"I don't know."

"He finished his walk," I say, "and then he went back home and took a nice warm bath and went to bed."

Now we're at the brink of revelation, and she knows it. She flattens her palms on the table and leans toward me over the empty Pepsi bottle. Her face is only inches from mine.

"So if that's all he did," she whispers, "why was what he saw up in the sky important?"

I take my time. I lift the beer mug and suck down some warm draft, then I stare out the door of the Universal Bar toward the bus stop where an old lady stands waiting. She cradles a little pig in her arms.

I set the mug back down and let my eyes meet Anna's. "Because," I tell her, "it got old Copernicus started looking up."

The resort at Bachotek is primarily for faculty at Nicholas Copernicus University in Torun. We're here because an old friend who teaches there arranged for us to come. He says the university is having trouble keeping the place open, so the manager, or Kierownik, takes in paying guests from outside. As a favor to our friend, Kierownik has agreed to a discount. He's under the impression that I'm on sabbatical.

We eat all our meals in a large hall near the pier. Each family has its own table, decorated with a plastic rose in a green glass vase. Until last year, I've been told, the roses were real. Then Kierownik opted for what he calls a one-time expenditure.

Just now, at supper, there are fifteen or twenty people present. Anna waves at Milek, her opponent in the competitions Kierownik stages daily for the children. Milek hollers "Hello, hello." He can speak a little English. His dad once spent a semester at East Lansing.

Basia spreads butter on a slice of bread and lays a single slice of cheese across it. She hasn't been eating much for the last few days. She hasn't eaten much for several months.

"I got a note from Kierownik this afternoon," she tells me.

I glance across the hall at the table where he eats. He's attacking a plate of spiced cabbage and sausage, his jowls flushed red from the effort. He doesn't look as if he's ever missed a meal. My friend in Torun says that right after martial law, when the shortages were at their worst, you could always eat pork for dinner at Bachotek. Kierownik, according to my friend, used to know all the local party functionaries. Now he knows all the priests. But mostly, I suspect, he knows himself, and he's a man who likes meat.

I say, "I had a coach back in Tennessee who used to eat like that."

"You can probably guess what the note was about."

"One time, at a Crystal on the way home from a road game, he ate thirteen burgers. Can you believe that?"

"I could believe anything," she says, "about somebody from Tennessee."

"Even me?"

"No," she says. "Not you. Not anymore."

"My boundaries have been determined?"

"Yes, and you've got some jagged borders."

This seems to me a fairly accurate assessment. I recall having made a similar judgment about myself not long after she met me, but she discounted it at the time.

"I assume his note was pleasant?"

"Extremely. He politely inquired how much longer we planned to be staying."

I blow a stage-sigh out so loudly that Milek's father looks our way. "Onward Spartans," I say and wave at him.

If he understood me, he doesn't let on. He smiles, nods, and goes back to eating supper.

"I was afraid," I tell Basia, "that the note had suggested we pay up and take off."

"That's what it was doing," she says. "But you know that, don't you?"

"The thought crossed my mind, but I managed to chase it away."

"Can't we pay him?" Anna says.

"Of course we can," we both say.

"That's good," she says. Her bangs sweep low, hiding one eye. "I mean, I think he's awfully nice."

Afterwards, walking up the hill toward the house, she stays several paces ahead of us, almost as if she knows we need a little extra space.

"You're going to have to call California," Basia says.

You can't call anyplace from here. The other day we went to the office and attempted to call Torun, and it was more than four hours before the operator phoned back. Then we learned we'd reached a wrong number.

"From Bachotek?" I say. "That's impossible."

"That's why you like it here," she says.

"That's not the whole story," I tell her.

"What is the whole story?"

"I don't know the whole story," I tell her. "I remember a few scenes from the beginning, and the middle is fresh in my mind. As far as the ending goes, I'm blind."

She may yell, I think. She may yell like she did before I agreed to leave Fresno, when I lay on the couch all day long every day, the paper open on my chest, headlines screaming nasty news about the state budget. She may pull a branch off a tree and rake my face. She may beg me to jump in the lake.

Instead she takes my hand in one of hers and leans against me. When I travel from one continent to another, start eating different foods and bathing with locally produced soap, my odor, I've noticed, has a tendency to change, as if alien substances have altered my essence. Basia always smells the same. A little bit like apples, a little bit like wintergreen.

"You go to Torun and call," she says. "School starts in three weeks. If they haven't hired people back yet, they're probably not going to."

"And after I make the call," I say, "we'll know finally, beyond all doubt, exactly what to call ourselves. Temporarily laid off or permanently unemployed."

She pulls away from me. In the dusk her face hardens. "How about calling ourselves a family?" she says. "Did you ever think of that?"

"The Bachotek Olympics will now get under way."

Kierownik proceeds to prove it by jamming a round into the chamber of his pistol. The smallest kids, those in the two- and-three-year-old's groups, cover their ears and shriek. Anna pivots on one toe, Milek hops up and down like Ali used to do after entering the ring.

We're standing in a large shed not far from the dining hall. The shed has an asphalt floor and a tin roof, upon which we can hear the rain beating. There are no walls, and the wind blowing in off the lake is cold and gusty. Milek's father and I stand near the kids, hugging ourselves, even though we're both wearing windbreakers.

"First event," Kierownik says, raising his pistol, "is the ten-meter dash. Two- and three-year-olds line up at the chalk mark."

The rest of us stand there and watch the confusion that results when Kierownik fires the pistol. One little boy starts crying and runs up the hill toward the houses. A girl turns and runs toward the lake. A few of the others take one or two tentative steps over the line and then stop. One kid, a plump little boy in red pants and green suspenders, gets off cleanly with the shot and waddles all the way across the finish line.

"A few years ago," Milek's father says, "I would have said that we had just watched a future first secretary."

"What do you say today?"

"Today," he says, "I say that we have just seen a young investment banker achieve glory in his first ten-meter race. You'll notice that he appears to be the least athletic of all the contestants assembled?"

"Also," I say, "the one least prone to distraction."

Milek could easily beat Anna, but as usual he refuses to do it. They run as if they're melded at the waist, bolting from the chalk line in unison and crossing the finish side by side.

Cheeks red, chests heaving, arms around each other's shoulders, they approach us, babbling a steady stream of Polish, which I can understand if I want to. Right now I choose not to, I let the words merge with the drumming on the roof, with the sound of wind whipping through the pines.

At breakfast this morning, Kierownik passed out papers he'd picked up earlier in Torun—*Gazeta Wyborcza, Polityka, Zycie Warszawy,* and just for Basia and me, the *Warsaw Voice,* an English-language weekly that averages about four grammar mistakes and two misspelled words per column inch. I thanked him but didn't open it. Basia did. The first thing to catch her eye was an ad for a copy editor.

"The successful applicant," she read, "will be a native Pole with writing and editing skills in both English and Polish and a thorough knowledge of Polish ways and customers."

"I guess they mean customs," I said.

"I guess they do."

"I guess you think you might fit the bill?"

"Somebody has to fit some bill," she said.

"What bill do you think I fit?"

"I don't have an opinion. You're the only one who can decide that."

"Funny to hear you say so," I said. "I don't feel like I've got the slightest control over it."

"If you don't have, who does?"

"A bunch of gray-haired guys in Sacramento."

She closed the *Warsaw Voice* and laid it down next to her teacup. "Yesterday afternoon," she said, "I did a little reading in one of your Shelby Foote books."

"Yeah? Did you check out the stuff on Vicksburg?"

"Actually, I did," she said. "I looked up the guy you mentioned. Pemberton. He had an interesting career. He was born in the North, but he married a woman from the South and fought for the Confederacy."

"You're saying I ought to fight for Poland?"

"Don't be a smartass."

"You're saying you want to fight for Tennessee?"

She stared at me as if I were the smallest form of life yet discovered.

"Well, if you're saying that I ought to fight for California," I said, "you can damn well forget it. It wasn't even in the Confederacy."

She picked up her fork. I didn't think she'd jab me with it, but I wasn't absolutely certain.

"After Pemberton surrendered Vicksburg," she said, "he was vilified throughout the Confederacy. There were those who actually suggested he'd lost the city and his army on purpose. Jefferson Davis didn't think so, but he couldn't risk giving him another command. So Pemberton resigned his commission as a lieutenant general and spent the rest of the war as a colonel of artillery."

It seemed only fitting at that moment to tunnel under her. It felt like the *thematic* thing to do. Besides, when you've sunk as low as I have, the only way you can move is by burrowing.

"That's in the second volume of the trilogy," I said. "If you'd looked into the third, you'd discover that Foote's final mention of John C. Pemberton occurs in connection with George Stoneman's raid on Salisbury, North Carolina. Guess what? J. C. surrendered again. Gave up every single piece of artillery he had, every last shell, all his powder and his fuses. What sort of bill would you say he fit?"

Anna fits the bill of Olympic champion, at least as it's defined by Kierownik. In Kierownik's Olympics you get to mount the podium if you show up and stick around. While Milek's father and I stand by shivering, she and Milek record broad jumps of almost two meters, they hurl the frisbee at least three times that far. They complete the high hurdles—two overturned red buckets in the middle of the ten-meter course—in just under five seconds, breaking the old Bachotek record.

"And that record," Kierownik says, waving his pistol and causing nervous looks on the faces of the smaller kids, "was set way back when the president of our country was still soldering wires together in the bellies of boats in Gdansk."

Every Thursday afternoon there's an art class, conducted by a watercolorist from Torun. The kids gather in the dining hall and practice drawing and painting under his supervision, and in the evening the results are displayed on the wall near the kitchen and analyzed by Kierownik while the rest of us eat. The artist who runs the classes says he thinks Anna has talent, though it's really too early to tell. Predictably, Anna's started saying she wants to be an artist too. When she asks me what I wanted to be at age five, I tell her I wanted to be a historian. That's true, as far as it goes. What I don't tell her is that I didn't want to be some of the other things I am. Unemployed, for instance. Incapable of supporting a wife who gave up a job she liked so she could come and live with me.

Basia has promised to take Anna to the class today, but

before she goes outside, where Anna's waiting in a fine gray drizzle, she says, "There's just one thing I want to say."

I'm sitting at the table, warming my feet in the heat from the electric radiator. I'm thinking that I've always loved rain. When I was a kid in Chattanooga, we lived on the side of Lookout Mountain, right above the Moccasin Bend. From there I could look straight down on the Tennessee, and when it was raining, I'd watch the river's rippling surface for hours, feeling snug and secure in my bedroom, thinking how lucky I was to be dry and warm, up there on the mountain rather than down in the cold deep river. Probably, if I want to be truthful about it, I've always feared falling into that river or one just like it. But the rain that swells the rivers is a longtime friend.

"You can either go to Torun tomorrow and call California or not," Basia says. "It's up to you. But Anna and I are leaving here."

"Going where?"

"Hopefully, somewhere with you. Either here or there. But we're moving out. Come Saturday morning we're starting our forward march."

I glance out the window at Anna. She's wearing the pink raincoat. She stands underneath a tree, getting dripped on and studying the ground.

"You've told her," I say.

"Of course I have. She's started thinking this is her home. It's not. It's a resort. Normal people stay here for a week or two. We've been here since June."

"You wanted to come to Poland."

"I wanted to get you *moving*. I wanted to get you off the goddam couch."

"You could have just dragged me up to Carmel."

"I wanted to be someplace where I can take care of Anna if I have to. Here I know how to get by." She opens the door, and cold air rushes in. "Other people have lost their jobs," she says. "Did it turn them into plants?"

I watch while they slog down the hill toward the dining hall. The voice in my head is speaking Polish, and for once I can't seem to jam it. It tells me that of course Basia's right. Other people learn to call themselves by more than one name, they learn to do more than one thing. Baseball players dip below the Mendoza line and pitch in with the used-car salesmen, janitors, restauranteurs. First secretaries become investment bankers. Leonardo was a brilliant artillerist, Walt Whitman made a marvelous nurse. Jimmy Carter's a hell of a carpenter.

Hit men turn preachers, preachers turn pushers. A priest from Torun stopped the Earth and moved the sun.

At supper Basia's silent, her motions brisk and businesslike. She butters Anna's roll, she pours hers and Anna's cups full of tea. Mine is left for me to fill. I pour it about half full, though I know I probably won't drink it. I want to get a good night's sleep. The bus to Torun leaves Tama Brodzka at 6:45, so I'll start the day with a long walk through wet woods. I'll have an even longer walk, I imagine, tomorrow afternoon coming back.

Toward the end of the meal Kierownik rises. He taps the side of a glass with his spoon, clears his throat, and gestures at the rear wall where the drawings from this afternoon hang.

"Ladies and gentlemen," he says, "it's time once again

to examine the creations of our young artists. Judging from their past efforts, I would say there's an excellent chance some of them will have their work displayed in Warsaw one day or maybe even in New York or the cities of the American West." He nods briefly at Anna, whose cheeks immediately redden.

He starts with the drawings of the little kids, the two- and three-year-olds. "Here," he says, pausing before the first picture, in which two skewed circles, one slightly larger than the other, overlap, "we have a metaphorical representation of September 1, 1939. The artist titillates us with his title—'Big Ball, Little Ball'—but it's clear to any informed observer that the Big Ball in the drawing is Hitler's Germany, and the Little Ball is Poland. The Big Ball is eating the Little Ball, but the deformation of the Big Ball—notice its squiggly borders, achieved by a very deft manipulation of the pencil—tells us that the Little Ball is already causing the Big Ball severe gastric disturbance. Here, of course, the artist comments upon the valiant efforts of the Polish army in the initial resistance to Hitler's war machine and at the same time skillfully foreshadows the Warsaw Uprising. The artist is both genius and patriot, and we marvel at the depth, the pure *historicity* of his vision."

He works his way through the whole series of drawings, spicing his analyses with references to Pilsudski, the Piast Dynasty, the Miracle on the Vistula, the Pope and the Black Madonna. Milek has drawn a turtle, which Kierownik says is nothing less than a symbol for contemporary post-Communist Poland: "slowly, inexorably putting herself back onto the right track."

Finally he comes to Anna's picture. It's a drawing of

the Three Bears. They're holding hands, and she's arranged them by height. The biggest of the bears wears an orange sweatshirt on which Anna has written VOLS— a year ago, we went to see Tennessee play UCLA at the Rose Bowl, and she must have seen such sweatshirts in the crowd. The middle bear is wearing a blowsy skirt. Anna's colored it red, black, green and gold, in imitation of Krakowian folk design. She has dolls that wear dresses like that, and she saw a Krakowian dance group a few weeks ago in Torun.

The third bear is just a bear. She's naked, if you want to put it that way. The most striking thing about her is that half her fur is white, and half her fur is black. The eye on the black side's white, the eye on the white side's black. It's as though she's part Polar bear, part Smoky bear, and thoroughly, unforgettably schizophrenic.

Kierownik, for a moment, seems troubled. He jams his hands in his pockets. His tongue pokes his jaw, as if probing for a weak spot. I measure the distance from where I'm sitting to the door, wondering how long it would take me to traverse it.

Then inspiration strikes him, you can see his eyes light up.

"Threeness," he says solemnly. "The Trinity. Its universal application. The utter indivisibility of it. Its importance in Poland and beyond."

It's my turn to put Anna to bed, so I climb the stairs to the attic. As soon as I slide under the covers, she says, "Daddy, tell me a story."

Lying there beside her in the dark, while the rain

drums down and tree branches rub the roof, I realize I'm tired of telling stories, because stories, unlike history, need to have endings. And for me right now endings are a problem.

"A thousand years ago tonight," I say, hearing the sudden sound of Basia slamming a door down below, the wheels of a suitcase squeaking on the floor, "the king of Poland rode through these woods in a heavy rain just like the one that's falling now. He rode a big white horse. Beside him, on two more white horses, rode his wife and his daughter."

"The queen," Anna says, "and the princess."

"That's right," I say. "They'd ridden a long way that day. They had crossed the Vistula at daybreak, and they'd kept on going until they came to these woods and saw the lake and here on the hill above it a shelter. And when the king saw the shelter, he decided they would stop for the night."

"Why were they riding through the woods?" she says.

"They were fleeing a hostile army. The king's army had fought a battle against the foe and lost, and then the army had deserted the king. And the king was trying to make sure he and the queen and the princess got away to someplace safe."

"And when he saw the shelter here on the hill," she says, "he believed he'd found that place?"

"At least for the meantime," I say. "For that night, at least, he knew it was safe."

"And later?"

"Later," I say, "he might not get to be king."

"Did he know that?"

"You bet he did. He knew that one day soon someone

else might decide to be king, and then he'd just be an ordinary person."

"Was he mad?"

"Not at all. He'd just about decided he was tired of being king anyhow. He was always fighting wars, some of which he'd started and some of which he hadn't, and he was always having to ride that big white horse, and the truth was horses scared him, and he didn't like the way they smelled."

She cuddles up close to me, so close I can feel her heart beating. "So what happened?" she says.

"That night? Nothing much. He and the queen and the princess went inside the shelter up here on the hill and they ate supper and got ready to put the princess to bed."

"Did the king put her to bed?"

"Sure enough," I say. "It was his night. And do you know what the princess said when he lay down beside her?"

"What?"

"The princess said, 'Tell me a story.'"

"And did the king do it?" she says, already sounding groggy.

"He did," I say. "This was the story he told her. 'Many years from now,' the king said, 'on a rainy night just like this one, a royal family found themselves up here on this hill. They didn't know how they'd gotten here. They had materialized, more or less, out of the air. That was how people traveled then,' he told her. 'One moment they were one place, one moment they were someplace else. In the course of their lives kings and queens and princesses lived in many different castles and ruled many different domains, some large, some small, some so tiny you could scarcely call them kingdoms at all. Sometimes,' the king said, 'a king might be a subject for a while, he might be an ordinary foot soldier, he might be a baker, a watchmaker, a puppeteer, the court fool. It wasn't always given to a king to rule.

" 'That night,' the king said, 'when the royal family went to bed, the princess asked the king to tell a story. And so he lay down beside her. And do you know what he said?' "

"No," she mumbles.

" 'The king said, "A thousand years ago tonight, the king of Poland rode through these woods in a heavy rain just like the one that's falling now. He rode a big white horse. Beside him, on two more white horses, rode his wife and his daughter. They were fleeing a hostile army." ' "

She isn't moving, so after a minute or two, I decide she's asleep. But when I start to crawl out of the bed, she says, "Daddy?"

"What, honey?"

"I can't tell what's real in that story."

I almost tell her that I don't know either, that I don't know what's real in this story or in any other. But an answer like that won't satisfy her.

"What do you think's real?" I ask her.

She reaches up and pulls my head back down onto the pillow. Her eyes are open wide, and they're neither black nor white. In the darkness they look gray.

"The night," she whispers, "and the hill and the lake. And the king and the queen. And the princess and the rain."

Sleet

WHAT SHE remembers, in the time she allots for remembering, is how cold the house got in winter. She would question the authenticity of that recollection, since she thinks of Mississippi as a hot sultry place; but her sister, who is a year older than she is, remembers those winters the same way. "It must have been the wind," her sister says. "Remember, there was that big empty field to the west?"

"I thought it was south of the house," Kendra says.

"It was west," her sister says. "On the other side of the road. The wind just came howling straight across that field, and I don't think the windows and the doors were well sealed."

They had space heaters. She remembers how she sometimes climbed out of bed, after Mary Jo had fallen asleep, and sat in front of the heater in their room, staring at the flames. The fire flickered behind radiants made of ceramic fire clay. The radiants were arched like the windows in the sanctuary at the Methodist church, and each one had many little diamond-shaped openings. She remembers sitting there in her pajamas for hours, watching the fire patterns, feeling warm, while a few feet away her sister slept. Sometimes, on nights when their father was home, she'd hear him roll over, the heavy weight of his body making the springs groan.

She remembers the traps they set out, the way they loaded them with stale cheese. Some of the traps were small, maybe three inches long. Others, the ones they placed in the attic, were almost a foot long. She knows that today she would not be capable of removing a furry little body from any sort of trap, no matter what size, but Mary Jo swears they both used to check the traps every morning and that when they found something dead in one of them, they took it out, tossed it into the green garbage barrel out back and reset the trap.

One night—one cold night—when they'd just gone to bed, they heard their mother scream. Both of them bolted for the door. Flinging it open, they saw their mother run naked from the bathroom, water dripping from her heavy breasts, water streaming down her back, her legs. Their father followed, a grayish ball dangling from his hand by what appeared to be a string.

He chased her into the living room and, while they watched, he cornered her near the television set. "It's just a mouse," he said. "A dead one. Don't you want to touch it? You like fur."

Their mother stood there dripping, shaking from cold or fear or both. Their father grinned. He took a step closer.

Suddenly the mouse twitched. Hollering, their father dropped it and jumped backwards.

She remembers the way the four of them stood there studying the mouse, which lay, almost flat, on the floor. Its neck had been crushed, the hair behind its head was matted with blood. Yet while they stood there, it twitched again.

You can be moving but dead, she remembers thinking. She believes this was the moment when she lost faith in boundaries, seeing life and the lack of it merge in a ball of fur.

Their father was gone so much because their farm, like a lot of small farms in the Delta, had failed and he'd taken a job selling dictionaries for a company based in Jackson. They still owned their house, though they'd lost the rest of the land, and they were staying there until he could afford to move them down. He came home every third or fourth weekend, bringing his samples with him, one big brown dictionary for grown-ups and a smaller red one for children.

He was renting a room in a big house on North State Street in Jackson. The people who lived there, he said, were all characters. He'd set Kendra on his knee when he came home and tell her about them.

"There's this one fellow that's the chaplain at Millsaps College," she remembers him saying, bouncing her, running his fingers through her curls. "He's about sixty years old now. You know what happens to you sometimes when you get to be about sixty?"

"You die?"

"Well, you could, but there's other less drastic stuff that happens."

"Like what?"

"You could lose your teeth."

"*I've* lost a tooth," she says. She opens her mouth to re-mind him of the gap there.

"Yeah, but you'll grow another one," he says. "When you're sixty and you lose them, that's it. All you can do is get fake teeth, and that's what Reverend Dooley went and did. But you know what happened the other Sunday?"

When she turns around to say *what?* her face grazes his. It's rough, stubbly. She wonders now if that's why stubble on a man's cheek never bothers her. Mary Jo says she can't stand it. Most women can't.

"Reverend Dooley was up preaching his sermon at the campus chapel, talking about sin and damnation, and he got carried away. He started pounding the pulpit and shaking his head, and the next thing he knew, his den-tures—that's his fake teeth—were flying through the air. He said they landed right in the organist's lap. He claims he's fixing to retire."

He tells her about Hardy the mechanic. Hardy's wife doesn't like him anymore, he says, so he's had to move into the boarding house. Hardy has problems at work. Her father tells her that the other day Hardy forgot to tighten the oil plug on somebody's Rolls Royce, a car that costs thousands and thousands of dollars, and the lady who owns the car drove it onto the highway and all the oil emptied out and the engine caught fire. Hardy gets grease on people's brake shoes and when they try to stop their cars they have wrecks.

"Hardy's a mess," he tells her. "Hardy hasn't had a whole lot of success."

She asks him what success is. The black satchel he

totes his samples in is standing by his chair. He reaches into the bag and pulls out the red dictionary, the one that's meant for kids. He flips pages until he finds the entry.

" 'Success,' " he says, " 'when the plans one has made work out.' "

"Have you had a lot of success?"

"I guess I've had my share."

He says it in what she will come to think of as a matter-of-fact way. It's as if the statement is a straight line running through the middle of his life, like the center stripe on a highway, separating what has worked out from what hasn't. He says it as if he thinks that, on the whole, things have balanced.

In her recollections, when she's sitting on his knee, listening to him and occasionally asking questions, Mary Jo and her mother are somewhere close by, in the house certainly, though never visible. It's possible that they're in the kitchen. Today Mary Jo is a terrible cook, at least as bad as Kendra; both of them prefer to eat out, and most nights they do. But Kendra remembers that at one time Mary Jo liked to help her mother cook, and she remembers that her mother cooked a lot of different things and cooked them well, particularly on those weekends when their father came home.

Her mother was at that time a woman who still dressed well, who never went out in the morning until she'd had a bath and put on a nice dress. The pictures taken in those days suggest that she dressed conservatively. Her skirts are long and full. The snapshots are black and white, so colors are hard to distinguish, but it doesn't look like she favored loud shades. She's never wearing a lot of makeup in those photos. What she is wearing, more often than not, is a frank friendly smile. She sang in the choir at the Methodist church, and she had friends, other women who always stopped and spoke to her when she and Kendra and Mary Jo went to shop in the Piggly Wiggly. They talked about the things women talked about then—about the need for a traffic light out on 82, the prices of various foods, the new toupee the choir director had worn last Sunday. They talked for hours, it seems like, though it couldn't have been that long.

Every now and then, a really good friend would glance down at her and Mary Jo and then lean close to their mother, her hand held up by her mouth like a shield, and the friend would say something in a low voice. Their mother would glance at them too, and then she'd shield her mouth and lean toward her friend and say something back. And afterwards, when Kendra—never Mary Jo— would ask what they'd been talking about, their mother would say, "Oh, we were just discussing some folks that we know."

"Who?"

"Just some people," their mother would say, paying most of her attention to the shopping cart, which she always pushed down the middle of the aisle, even if someone else was coming toward her; she would hew to the center until the last second, then veer reluctantly off to one side. "Just some people who are having hard times."

The beginning of their own hard times is difficult to place.

Kendra knows when she became aware that something

drastic had happened. But she also knows that before the drastic event, there were other, more subtle indications of what Mary Jo calls "drift."

"It's like that Honda I had a few years ago," Mary Jo says. As an adult, she's developed deep attachments to all of the cars she's owned; her estranged husband, with whom she's had an on-again, off-again relationship for almost thirty years, is himself a car salesman. "It got to the point," Mary Jo says, "where you couldn't steer that car at all. The second I realized it had a problem, I knew I'd been seeing signs of it for more than a year."

How long Kendra was aware of similar signs in the life of their family is hard to say. When the bank told her father that it would have to seize most of his land and all of his farm equipment, he didn't seem particularly distraught. The night he came home with the news, they all sat out on the front porch, eating fresh strawberries from their garden and laughing.

"Maybe," she hears her father say, pink juice dripping down his chin, "I'll become an evangelist." He winks at their mother. "Don't you think I'd make a good one? The main thing an evangelist needs is the ability to believe the stories he tells. I can do that. The only other thing he needs is a little bit of charm."

There's a picnic table on the front porch—a table that appears in many photos—and that's where they're sitting. She's on the bench beside her father, Mary Jo and her mother are across the table. It's raining, big drops thudding on the roof like rocks. Their mother reaches over to clasp their father's hand.

"You could charm the fur off a fox," she says. "You could charm anything off anybody."

"I could be a truck driver," her father says.

Her mother says, "Gitty-up-go."

He snaps his fingers. "I know," he says. "Remember what a curve I had in high school? I could take up pitching. I'm still young enough to make the major leagues. Wouldn't you girls like to see me on TV? Imagine how I'd look on the mound at Yankee Stadium. Dizzy'd be calling my name out every week."

For a long time Kendra offered up the memory of that evening to herself as evidence that things were still okay at that point. But after a while, the evening became evidence of something else altogether. Every occupation her father facetiously proposed involved travel. Each one would have taken him away from her and Mary Jo and their mother, just as surely as the one he finally hit on.

When he first took the job selling dictionaries, he phoned every couple of days. Later the phone calls became infrequent. Later still, to save money—toward buying a house in Jackson, he said, a place where they could all live together—he suggested they have their own phone removed. Their mother reluctantly agreed.

As for their mother, Mary Jo says she's like Nixon: the question is what did she know and when did she know it. But in Kendra's mind, the question is not what their mother knew and when she knew it. The question is *how* she knew it. Kendra sees her knowing as a dark heavy thing, a coldness that crept into her and made it hard for her to move.

At a certain point in her recollections, her mother begins to move in slow motion. Lying in bed beside Mary Jo or sitting on the floor in front of the space heater, Kendra hears her mother's footsteps in the kitchen. The interval between one footstep and the next starts to seem absurdly long, and as she waits to hear it, she sees her mother's ragged pink slipper descending slowly, almost as if a parachute were attached to it, asserting drag. Meals take longer for their mother to fix; dinner, which at that time they called supper, begins to come from cans and boxes. Washing dishes, she sometimes pauses, a saucer in one hand, a soapy sponge in the other, to stare out the window at the field across the road.

One day she walks out onto the porch while they're doing their homework; they've just returned from school. A storm is banking up in the west. "A cloud's coming," she says. It moves in fast, sudden gusts of wind rake the pecan trees, brown-hulled nuts shower down, and then the rain itself. It's heavy rain, Mississippi rain, silver sheets that ripple like stage curtains.

The storm only lasts ten or twelve minutes. But there's a lot of thunder and lightning, and the whole time it's going on, their mother is out there on the porch. Kendra believes they must have worried about her, that they would have begged her to come in unless they somehow knew that she needed, right then, to be alone with the wind.

Afterwards, she walks in and says, "Let's go get in the truck."

They're using the truck because their father has the car. The truck is an ancient black International pickup with running boards like you see on the cars in gangster movies. Starting it can be a problem, but today it cranks right up.

Kendra's next to the door, Mary Jo is in the middle. Their mother doesn't say where they're going; in fact, the way Kendra remembers it, she doesn't say a word for the entire trip, and for once Mary Jo can't contradict her because Mary Jo says the trip didn't take place. Or to be more precise, Mary Jo says the trip took place later—at least three months later, possibly more—and she says it took place on a Saturday morning.

In Kendra's version it's late afternoon, probably the third or fourth week in October. From the distance of forty years and two thousand miles, everything appears in soft focus. The barn beside the highway lacks line and definition; a red farmhouse, set farther back, bleeds color. There's cotton in the field, there must be. White splotches appear in the picture.

Their mother parks the truck in a gravel lot before a small brick building at the edge of a field. Other pickup trucks are parked here too. A couple of men wearing muddy overalls are standing in front of the building, gesturing at the sky, then at the ground. They must be farmers. They were probably out in the fields picking cotton when the storm hit.

Their mother gets out of the truck. The men stop talking. They stare at her. She walks past them, into the store.

Because that's what it is: a store. On the window, white letters with red borders spell LIQUOR. Their mother is inside for a couple of minutes. While she's in there, the two muddy farmers look at the pickup truck, at Kendra and her sister, and then they shake their heads.

Their mother comes out toting a brown paper sack. She gets into the truck and starts it, and they turn around and go back.

For a long time Kendra believes that her mother has

driven some distance away from home in order to avoid being seen by anyone who knows her. This, in an odd way, offers comfort, further proof of propriety.

Then, years later, while she's prowling around the library at UCLA, her mind half numb from trying to focus on the note cards she's been filling out for five or six hours, the title on the spine of a book catches her attention. *Fevers, Floods and Faith.* It's a history of Sunflower County, Mississippi. Sitting down and flipping through it, she learns that the county she grew up in was dry until 1968.

What her mother must have done that day was drive across the line into another county. What her mother must have done, even then, when she was still going to church on Sunday and saying amen and other women still spoke to her in the aisle at Piggly Wiggly, was buy her booze the first place she could find it.

There are certain things, Kendra understands, that perceptive men figure out about her.

A perceptive man learns that when he's with her, he's the only other person in her world; when he's not with her, he can expect to feel as if for her he no longer exists. Phone calls will go unanswered; messages will seldom be returned. From time to time, she will simply disappear.

Many of the men she's known have been married. A few have tried to leave their wives and children for her. But perceptive men know or figure out that you can't leave your wife and children for Kendra.

Children—she knows this from experience—feel it when you pose a threat to them. They feel the threatening fact of your existence, even if they never know your face. They feel you in the faraway stares on the faces of those who matter most.

Children—especially the children of the men she knows—love Kendra, to Kendra they come running. They perch on her knee while she whispers to them. Tiny fingers find their way into her hair, little arms wrap themselves around her neck.

People shake their heads. It's a pity, they say, that she never had a few kids of her own.

The Christmas tree looks threadbare. Her father notices it the moment he walks in.

He's been gone again, this time for almost a month. It's a few days till Christmas. They picked the tree up the other day with their mother. It's a cedar tree, and except for a single string of lights and four or five glass ornaments, there's nothing on it.

There's not much under it either. Two packages for Kendra and two for Mary Jo and one for their father. They're not expecting a lot this year, they know times are hard.

"This tree's almost naked," their father says. "This tree belongs in *Playboy*."

Not too long ago their mother would have come back with something snappy like *It's too skinny for that*. Now she says nothing. She's sitting on the couch, drinking hot tea from a white cup that has a drawing of a magnolia on it. The tea smells funny. Kendra knows it does because sometimes her mother leaves that cup standing around, and more than once Kendra has picked it up and sniffed it.

"Who wants to go with me to town," their father says, "and get some decent duds for this tree?"

Her voice is the only one that says *I do*.

It's raining again, and the rain is cold, so cold that her father says he bets it will turn into snow or, at the very least, sleet. Sleet is something she knows about then, though the word will soon disappear from her active vocabulary. Words like *surf* and *freeway* will replace *sleet* and *defoliant*. Her surroundings are about to change, the blacktop road she's riding on will at times seem so far away that her distance from it can't be measured; at other times she'll travel down it again, through cold rain turning into something hard and icy, through darkness that seals her up forever into these moments with her father.

The wipers squeak back and forth across the windshield. Her father keeps his eyes on the road. He's a careful driver. Tonight they travel slow.

"Doing okay in school?" he says.

"I'm doing fine."

"You'll always do fine."

The way she will remember that line, the first word is italicized.

"You're an awfully smart little girl," he says. He reaches across the seat and takes her hand in his and gives it a squeeze.

"Mary Jo's smart too," she says.

"She sure is. But she's smart in a different way."

"What way am I smart?"

"You're smart in ways that may not always make life easy."

The lack of syntactical clarity in this statement is not, she knows now, what causes him to pause for several minutes. When he speaks again, he says, "I mean, let's think about explorers. You know what explorers are?"

"People that discover something?"

"Yeah. Sometimes what they discover causes them trouble. You probably haven't heard of a guy named Galileo, but he's the fellow who pretty much proved once and for all that the Earth was not the center of creation. And he got into hot water for saying so. People thought he was way out of line."

Her father says he thinks she might be an explorer. He says she may not ever discover new continents or galaxies, but she may discover other things that people might not want to know. She may not even want to know them herself, he says.

Through the rain, the lights of town, slanted and distorted, begin to appear. Where the road crosses the highway, there's a red light. They stop there, waiting for the light to turn green.

When the light turns green, they'll turn into the highway. They'll drive along the highway for a mile or so, take a right onto Sunflower Avenue, and head for downtown. Once there, they'll park on the street, in front of Piggly Wiggly, right beneath one of several big candy canes that dangle over the sidewalks at Christmas. They'll get out of the car and hurry through the rain to Woolworth's, and they'll rush inside and buy two strings of Christmas lights, a package of tinsel, and a box of ornaments made of colored glass.

But before all of that happens, while they're still waiting for the light to change, her father has one more thing to say.

One day, he says, in the not-too-distant future, he'll be

going away. He might be gone a lot longer this time, so long that Kendra's mother and Mary Jo may think he's never coming home.

"But you won't think that, will you?" he says.

She recalls shaking her head.

"That's good," he says. "Just remember that you're an explorer. It just so happens that I am too. We'll find each other again, you and me, and then we'll find your mother and Mary Jo. Just as sure as that red light up there's about to turn green."

The light changes colors, and then they're gone.

And then, several days later, on December 27, a date she and Mary Jo never disagree about, she wakes to find him gone.

A couple of hours later, around ten o'clock, he's really gone.

The Mississippi Highway Patrol car that she remembers is a black-and-white creation. Mary Jo says it was blue, that the car Kendra has in mind is the one Barney Fife drove on *The Andy Griffith Show*. Kendra doesn't say so, but she knows it isn't a car from TV she has in mind. The truth is that she sees the entire scene in black and white, so there's no other color the highway patrol car could be.

The state trooper climbs the front steps. He's wearing a raincoat—black in the picture—and the raincoat is wet and shiny. Her mother carries her cup to the front door. She's been drinking from it all morning, the funny-smelling tea.

She opens the door, and there the trooper stands, a

wide-brimmed hat, wet also, in his hands. He asks if she's Mrs. Nelson.

They're behind her now, Kendra and her sister; Mary Jo clings to her mother's bathrobe. Kendra keeps her hands to herself. She touches no one, no one touches her.

For the longest time their mother fails to answer. Later, it will occur to Kendra that she's had to consider the question, whether or not she's really Mrs. Nelson; it's almost as if in this moment she's become aware that her identity has changed.

She nods, but the nod is something less than a yes.

The trooper says he's sorry to bear bad news. The rest passes in a gray blur, one fact colliding with another: how 49 South has a glaze on it this morning, the trouble some motorists have had with visibility; the way her father lost control of his car, how he slid out of his lane and into the other, what happened when he hit the bridge abutment. How very sorry the state trooper is, how he wishes he had better news to bring her and her beautiful girls.

"They look so much like you," he says, this big awkward man who is the first among many men to express sympathy for their mother, to be moved by the sight of this lonely woman, these fatherless girls.

In the next five years Kendra lives in six states, in rented houses, rundown apartments and once, on the outskirts of Freeport, Texas, in a motel. Her mother moves westward, drawn on by men who always seem to be headed in that direction. The last one leaves them within sight of the Pacific, in a walk-up apartment in Long Beach.

Her mother quits going to church. She works from time to time as a waitress, at other times as a desk clerk at motels. She loses one job after another, very often for drinking at work. She's happiest when there are men around to take care of her. A lot of them do but only for a while.

When she looks back on this period in her life, Kendra remembers walking home from school—walking from many different schools, to many different homes. She remembers some of the sights she saw along the way: the barbecue stand beside the street in Freeport, where the woman who did the cooking sometimes motioned her in and offered her french fries and a running commentary on the lives of the characters in *General Hospital* and *The Edge of Night;* a junkyard in Phoenix, the tiger-striped cat who prowled there, crawling among the wrecks in search of mice; a drive-in in Banning, California, where teenagers parked for hours, rock and roll blaring from their radios, the guys trading innocent threats, the girls jumping out of one car and into another, giggling, their ponytails flying.

But mostly what she remembers from that period is the walks she took with her father. She met him almost daily, he had never been more real. He turned up in every city she lived in. She told him of the various discoveries she had made since that morning when Highway 49 glazed and he strayed from the southbound lane. She told him that by Christmas of the first year in Jamestown, only 32 out of more than 100 colonists were still alive; they'd built their village in a swamp, she said, and mosquitoes had bitten them and made them sick. She told him that Mozart had been a prodigy, that he'd composed music on the piano when he was only five years old.

The highest mountain in the world is in Asia, she said, the world's longest river is in Africa. The greatest lake is the Caspian Sea. The first chief justice of the Supreme Court was John Jay.

You weren't really selling those books, she said. You hadn't been selling them for almost three months. She told him how their mother loaded them both into the truck, how the truck quit in Belzoni and their mother got a garage mechanic to make it run by promising to come back on the weekend for a date. She told him Mary Jo looked the other way when they came to the bridge over the Yazoo River, but she and her mother saw the blue paint on the abutment, and her mother sobbed silently all the way to Jackson. She told him about waiting outside in the truck, while her mother carried his black satchel that contained the dictionaries into a little office within sight of the Capitol Dome, how she came out moments later, her face white and dead. *You can't trust a man,* she said, this woman who would spend the rest of her life entrusting herself and her girls to one man after another.

She told her father she believed the boarding house existed but only in his mind. She told him she believed that somewhere there was someone else, someone besides her mother, and that this was who he had gone to. She didn't know why he hadn't made it the last time.

Her father never answered, he never said a word, but answers were not what she sought. She poured herself out to him. In return he gave her his attention, and right then that was enough.

The year she turns fifty, she goes back.

It's January, and she's on winter break from the university where she teaches. She and Mary Jo fly into Memphis, rent a car and drive down into the Delta.

They spend the night at a Comfort Inn in Indianola, the town where they grew up. In the morning they eat breakfast at McDonald's. They drive through the downtown area—the Piggly Wiggly's gone now—then they cross the highway on a blacktop road that heads north.

It's a cold gray day; a brisk wind is blowing. In the fields, dead cotton stalks bend double. She remembers the way those stalks whistle when the wind blows hard. It's a sound she hasn't thought about in years.

These days a lot of the land is given over to catfish ponds. They see them now, muddy rectangles that spread out on both sides of the road, breaking the countryside up into watery sections.

There's a pond across the road from their house, where the empty field used to be. The field, as it turns out, was on the north side of the house, not the west or the south.

"We were both wrong," Mary Jo says.

Somebody has turned the front porch into a room and added on another structure to serve as a porch. There are trees all around, more than either of them remembers, pine trees as well as pecan. A Ford pickup is parked in the driveway.

A swing set stands in the yard. Near the front porch

there's a pink tricycle; a white basket is attached to the handlebars, red streamers dangle from the grips.

Looking at the house, Kendra wonders if the space heater remains in the bedroom where the little girl who owns that tricycle sleeps. She wonders if the child ever sits before the heater like she did.

Once again, for a few seconds, she lets herself remember the way the radiants split the fire into diamond-shaped bits. When she was two or three, each of those pieces seemed separate and distinct; she thought she was looking at many different flames, not a single burning thing.

Back then the world was new, and she believed, as children do, that lines possess the power to divide.

About the Author

STEVE YARBROUGH is Professor of English at California State University in Fresno. He is the author of other short story collections, including *Mississippi History* (University of Missouri Press).